THE BOUNTY HUNTER

The Bounty Hunter

George G. Gilman

NEW ENGLISH LIBRARY
TIMES MIRROR

An NEL Original
© George G. Gilman, 1974

✱

FIRST NEL PAPERBACK EDITION MAY 1974

✱

NEL Books are published by
New English Library Limited from Barnard's Inn, Holborn, London E.C.1.
Made and printed in Great Britain by Hunt Barnard Printing Ltd, Aylesbury, Bucks.

45001808 3

for
L.M.H.
owed so much

Chapter One

THE town was called Nuevo Rio but it was neither new nor stood anywhere near a river. Just a handful of single storey buildings of adobe and timber crouched around three sides of a plaza with the headless statue of a long dead military governor at its centre. A few houses, a store which sold everything or nothing depending upon what a customer was seeking, a cantina, a blacksmith, a livery and a bank. Nobody lived in the houses, and the business premises in Nuevo Rio provided the essentials and few luxuries required by the peons from the dirt farms in the surrounding country. Likewise the requirements of the infrequent travellers who came in off the trail – from Arizona less than five miles to the north or anywhere in the entire wedge of Mexico spreading out southwards beyond the jagged Sierra Madre Mountains.

For a traveller to make use of the cantina's crude accommodation for more than a single night was unusual: for an American to do so was unique in living memory.

But Adam Steele had been living in the tiny, spartanly-furnished room at the back of the cantina for so long – almost a month – that the local people had exhausted scope for conjecture and simply accepted his presence as a fact of life. His novelty as a stranger had worn off.

Steele felt neither novel nor unique as he sat at his usual corner table in the cantina. He felt nothing except drunk. Not falling down drunk. Not even unsteady drunk. Merely detached from his squalid surroundings as he licked salt, sipped tequila and chased the fiery spirit with tepid beer. He had achieved this state of being separate from the world beyond his own imagination on this third day in Nuevo Rio. At that time he was still something of an object of wonder to the local population and the withdrawal into himself had enabled him to ignore the eyes peering in at him through the windows and the surreptitious glances from the drinkers inside.

This achieved, his alcohol-sodden brain had been left free to work in isolation, unhindered by outside influences. Memories flipped out from the dark recesses of his mind and he was no longer in the fetid cantina of a forsaken town slowly dying amid parched Mexican mountains under a merciless sun. Instead, Virginia. Green and pleasant. Springtime warm. A plantation to which he was heir. His father. His friends. Good food and a sufficiency of alcohol. A girl. Laughter. The war!

During those first few days of hard drinking the war had always intruded on his thoughts too early. But he had willed himself to beat it. Learned to pace his memories so that the ugliness which had ended everything that was good in his life did not penetrate until late at night: when the sun was long down behind the mountain peaks and the stink of spluttering kerosene lamps filled the cantina. Then he would walk stiffly to the room at the back and stretch out beneath the rancid, dirt-stiffened blanket on the hard cot. Sleep veiled the past and in the morning a first drink would reactivate the residue of his vast intake of the previous day. And his life when it was good would once more be re-enacted on the stage of his mind.

'Señor.'

Steele's mind was jerked into the present at the sound of the single, soft-spoken word. He had been thinking about a Christmas party at the big plantation house: about how he had left the happy, laughing people to take a midnight ride across the snow carpeted fields on the big chestnut mare his father had given him as a present.

It was a rude awakening to reality: from a bygone age of black sky and crisply white land, of distant church bells ringing joyfully against the snow-muffled thud of hoofbeats and icy air permeated by the aromas of wood smoke and fresh horse sweat. Instantly, he was aware of today. The window shutters and door of the cantina were open and the harsh sunlight was dazzling even in refraction off the grey dust layered across the plaza. The only sounds in the world were of the blacksmith as he hammered at his anvil, the droning conversation of two men and the wheezy breathing of Manuel. The overheated air was heavy with the stink of stale alcohol, cheap cigar smoke and unwashed bodies.

'Yeah, Manuel?' Steele's black eyes were glazed as he raised his chin off his chest to look up at the cantina's owner and his lips hardly moved as he spoke.

Manuel – sixty-years-old, and looking taller than his five feet because of his emaciation – showed an expression of melancholy on his careworn features. Because of the grime and beard of more than a month's neglect it was difficult to read any kind of emotion in Steele's face.

'The money, señor,' Manuel said ruefully. 'It was all gone last night. I talk with my wife. We agree you have been good customer. I say to her that you have caused no trouble. I say that you may drink one more morning. For nothing. On the house as you Americanos say. It is midday now, señor. We are poor people. Cannot afford . . . '

His voice trailed off and he shrugged his painfully thin shoulders.

Steele blinked his eyes several times, like a man who had just woken up and was taking his bearings. Then he pressed himself very erect in the chair, stretching stiffened muscles.

'You shouldn't have done that, Manuel,' he said, his voice stronger and less slurred. 'You should have told me last night.'

Manuel shrugged again. His hollow-cheeked face was still mournful. 'In Mexico, we understand trouble, señor. We try to help, in the best way we can.'

Steele nodded and looked around him. The cantina was small, with just room for a sparsely stocked bar at the rear and half a dozen tables spread out in front. Manuel's wife stood behind the bar, as thin as and looking much older than her husband. Her liquid brown eyes held pity and she refused to meet Steele's gaze, fearful that he would resent such a feeling. On the far side of the room, two Americans sat at a table. Both were about thirty but were dissimilar in every other respect. One was open-faced and had the trappings of a drummer: Eastern suit complete with derby, a leather valise and a too-easy smile that made his eyes shine and showed very white teeth. The man seated across the table from him was half a head taller and much leaner. He wore a checked shirt and neckerchief and faded levis. A low-crowned, wide-brimmed hat hung down his back. Below the high forehead of a receding hairline he had a weathered face upon which a smile would seem out-of-place. He wore a tied-down holster with the butt of a Remington revolver curving out of it. The wooden grip had several notches in it.

Each man had a glass of flat beer in front of him. The drummer was talking enthusiastically as his potential customer listened absently, concentrating his attention on the open doorway he faced.

Little had changed since Steele had last taken notice of his surroundings. Then, Manuel and the women had been smiling, showing their pride that a gringo had given them a great deal of dollars and trusted them not to cheat him. And the other customers in the cantina had been four peons drinking mescal and worrying about whether they could afford the luxury.

'Thanks,' Steele said, getting to his feet. 'How long has it been?'

'You have been drunk almost a month, señor,' Manuel replied and his tone was now a mixture of relief and admiration. Relief that the man was prepared to accept the inevitable as calmly as he had his drinking: and admiration that he could drink so much for so long and still stand unaided.

The scraping of the chair legs drew the attention of the other two customers to their fellow American. The drummer showed a flicker of annoyance that his sales pitch had been interrupted. The taller man seemed faintly disgusted. Both found themselves looking at a slightly built man in his late twenties. He was a shade over five feet six inches tall and although slim there was something about him – the way he held himself, even when drunk – that indicated a higher than average degree of strength. Despite the long stubble and sweat-run crusting of dirt on his face, his regular features were seen to have a certain nondescript handsomeness. His mouthline was long and unaggressive, his nose was straight and coal black eyes surveyed his surroundings with an expression indicating that he brought no preconceived opinions to new experience. Prematurely grey hair, as unkempt as everything else about him, showed only faint traces of its former red colour. He was dressed in a filthy, once white shirt and dark grey pants. His riding boots were caked with mud dried as hard as cement. An incongruous note was struck by an odd kind of neckerchief hung around his throat and held together at the front by an overlapping of metal weights tied to two corners.

The disapproving eyes of the taller man also noticed something else which was strange about Steele – a slit at the seam of his right pants leg which ran for about four inches down the side of his calf.

'Look,' the dummer said, louder, to recapture the reluctant attention of the man sharing his table. 'Just look at it, uh?'

He lifted his valise from the floor and set it on the table.

The tall man sighed. 'Okay, looking won't cost me anything.'

Blessed with the optimism essential in his trade, the drummer brightened his smile and snapped open the valise. He reached a very white, soft-looking hand inside and brought out a sixgun. He put it on display, pressing the muzzle into the palm of one hand and the back of the butt into the other. The tall man's indifferent survey could thus take in a full profile of the oil-sheened weapon.

'It looks like a short barrelled forty-four calibre Starr,' the man said after a short glance. Then the plaza with its beheaded statue recaptured his attention.

'But it ain't,' the gun salesman responded.

Steele yawned and rubbed a hand over his face. The length and thickness of the bristles surprised him. But then he recalled what Manuel had said. Almost a month of nothing but drinking and sleeping. A man could halt time in his mind, but beyond his awareness natural progression continued.

'Didn't I eat at all?' he asked.

Manuel smiled. He had only one tooth, in the centre of his upper gum. 'Each midday and evening, señor. My wife, she cooked tortillas. I brought them with new drinks. Always you ate them, señor.'

Steele nodded, pleased there was a reason why he did not feel a painful hunger. 'I'd like to clean up.'

'Si, señor,' Manuel replied enthusiastically. 'My wife, she has put some hot water in your room. My razor is there, also. We hoped ... thought you would wish this.'

Steele rested a hand on Manuel's scrawny shoulder, then squeezed in a gesture of friendship. He turned and walked in a perfectly straight line towards the doorway at the end of the bar. At first he concentrated hard, but then tested his involuntary equilibrium. No stagger or sway. Manuel had exhausted his ability to be generous at a stage when Steele had drunk himself sober.

Not actually, he told himself as he began to shave in the tiny back room. For it was not possible to do that. His soberness, like the rest of his life over the past month, was all in his mind. He had been forced to face up to reality and the view was so bleak that his mind dictated the need for clear thinking. And clear thoughts made for deliberate actions. But it was easy to think he must walk straight and then do so. Simple to shave himself without nicking his flesh. He accomplished this sitting on the edge of the cot with the bowl of hot water on the floor and a broken piece of mottled mirror resting on his knees.

Then he took his sheepskin jacket from the doorless closet. And, from beneath the cot, he dragged out his rifle and blew the dust from it. The gun was an unusual one. A Colt Hartford sporting rifle with a revolving cylinder chambered for six .44 bullets. Its rosewood stock was slightly charred from exposure to a fire but the flames had not tarnished the gold plate with its inscription: TO BENJAMIN P. STEELE, WITH GRATI-TUDE – ABRAHAM LINCOLN.

Steele used his shirt cuff to polish the inscribed plate, then checked his other weapons which were a mixture of the conventional and the unusual. First he folded his right knee so that the slit in his pants leg gaped. He delved a hand inside and felt the

12

wooden handle of the knife protruding from the boot sheath. In the left hand pocket of his coat was a two-shot derringer. Stuck into the underside of the coat's right lapel was a long stick pin with an ornate head. Finally he fingered the weights in the corners of the scarf around his throat. Weights which turned the simple length of material into an instrument of death.

As he took his hat from a peg behind the door and set it on his head, he froze. A heavy frown lined the freshly-shaved skin of his face. Why had he run this automatic check over his weapons? A habit picked up as a Confederate officer during the longs years of the war between the States? Partly, perhaps. But the war was over now and he was a long way from any area where resentments and enmity still lingered on in an uneasy peace. And where was he, in fact? When his overworked memory flipped forward the answer to this, the whole span of a more recent past was revealed. He was in Nuevo Rio, Sonora. And he had checked his weapons so carefully because – just as in the war – his life could depend upon them. For with the ending of the war between the North and South, he had started another, more private one. He had been on the winning side this time, tracking down and killing the men who lynched his father. But he had killed others, too. One of them his best friend who placed his duty as a law officer above personal considerations.*

So Steele had come to Nuevo Rio to escape justice. And he had tried to drown the recent past in a gigantic jag: to forget what others had done to him and he had done to others. His automatic reflex actions upon returning to reality showed that Nuevo Rio had achieved nothing. The war had taught him how to kill and circumstances had moulded him into a killer without society's excuse of a nationalistic cause.

And, as he moved back out into the cantina he could feel no sense of shame. Regret that it had been necessary to kill Jim Bishop: nothing else. Even this not so strongly as on the long ride to Mexico. Just as time and alcohol had dulled the bitter edge of grief for his father. So perhaps Nuevo Rio had served some purpose after all.

The gun salesman was still making his pitch. He had stripped

* See – Steele: The Violent Peace.

13

the handgun and was in process of reassembling it, giving a running commentary which he had obviously learned by heart. The tall man was as unimpressed as ever as he sipped at his beer and stared fixedly out of the doorway. Manuel and his wife were both behind the bar now and they beamed with delight when they saw Steele emerge, his clean-shaven face emphasising the dishevelled state of his clothing.

'One more drink, señor,' Manuel greeted. 'On the house. To welcome you back to our world.'

He reached under the bar top and came up with a precious bottle of American bourbon. The tall man at the table turned to glance at Steele and betrayed nothing of what he thought about the partial transformation. Steele smiled and shook his head as he moved along the bar. He rested his rifle and coat on the scarred and stained top.

'I think I've had enough to last me a lifetime, Manuel,' he said.

The Mexican woman, who did not look quite so old when she was happy, spoke rapidly in Spanish. Manuel nodded several times in agreement.

'My wife say we should not think this way, because we have cantina. But we both happy you not drink any more, señor.'

More fast Spanish from the woman.

'My wife say, you like tortillas? On the house. Instead of drink.' He put the bourbon out of sight again, to await the next customer he considered worthy of it.

'Sounds good,' Steele replied.

The woman did not need a translation and she turned to go through a beaded curtain hung in an archway behind the bar. Steele turned sideways on to the bar to glance out through the doorway. With the sun at its midday peak the shadows were short, very black against the parched grey of the plaza and bleached adobe and timber of the buildings surrounding it. Two scrawny chickens scratched at the dust close to the base of the stucco figure of the military governor standing to headless attention. Immediately outside the cantina a horse was hitched to a rail. The animal looked as if it had been hard ridden and droning flies were giving it a bad time. Across the plaza a buggy was parked beneath the awning in front of the town's only store,

The buggy had a sign on top: IRA HOUGHTON – GUNS. Flies were also troubling the horse in the shafts, but at least the heat would not be so intense in the awning's shade. Next to the store was the blacksmith shop. The man had obviously been offered a good price for his labour to be working at this time of day. Then came the bank.

'I came in on a horse, didn't I?' Steele asked Manuel.

'Si, señor.' The single tooth went on display again. 'I put him in the livery stable for you. I have been paying my cousin each day. My cousin, sometimes he cheats. I make sure he does not cheat you, señor.'

'See how easy it is, sir?' Ira Houghton told the tall man as he finished fitting the gun back together again. 'Even a Colt takes longer.'

Manuel's wife brought out the tortillas and made an open-handed gesture which invited Steele to eat.

'I use a Remington,' the tall man replied sourly.

'I know that,' Houghton said quickly. 'I saw it. Surprised me. I thought Pinkerton men all carried Trantors.'

Steele stopped chewing on a mouthful of the greasy tortilla. Manuel saw his sudden change of mood and stopped smiling. His wife cocked her head to one side like a dog trying to understand something said to it.

'I use a Remington,' the tall man repeated in the same tone.

Steele rested his hip against the bar again to look towards the occupied table. Houghton was now getting a little irritated by the continued indifference to his product. The Pinkerton detective maintained his surveillance of the plaza. Steele resumed his meal, chiding himself for being a fool. Had the Pinkerton Agency been looking for him, the detective would have made his move earlier. Manuel showed his single tooth grin again and his wife sensed the momentary tension had evaporated.

The blacksmith stopped hammering and in the sudden stillness the sound of distant hoofbeats had an ominous quality. They were coming from the north, the horsemen riding down the long curve of dusty trail that dropped gently from a high plateau. There were dirt farms up on the plateau as well as in the arid valleys that cut away from Nuevo Rio in other directions. But the peons, if they had any riding animals at all, had

15

burros. The staccato sound which quivered in the hot afternoon air now was made by strong horses spurred into a fast gallop.

'Shut up!' the Pinkerton man said, very distinctly, as the drummer made a last ditch effort to gain his interest.

There was anger in the voice. But also a greater degree of strain than the minor irritation an insistent salesman should arouse. Steele finished the second tortilla and turned to place his back against the bar. As he did so, he noticed that Manuel and the woman were listening to the hoofbeats with something close to fear in their dark eyes. When Manuel began to speak to his wife in soft-voiced Spanish the words had a placating tone.

The riders did not slacken their pace until they rode into the plaza. Then, they reined hard. The horses reared and whinnied. Dust rose in a large grey cloud as the sounds of the abrupt halt were amplified by echo between the façades of the buildings. When the dust settled it could be seen that three men had ridden into town. All Americans, all in their early thirties and all showing signs of a long, hard ride. Stubbled faces with dirt plastered to the flesh by dried sweat. Dark coloured clothing powdered by grey dust. Beneath them, winded horses with bulging eyes and lathered flanks.

All three raked their hard, glinting stares around the plaza, controlling their mounts with knee pressure and a single hand on the reins. Their other hands were curled around the centres of balance of Henry rifles. Their survey completed, they swung out of the saddles in unison. A stucco sword hilt jutted from a stucco scabbard at the hip of the beheaded statue and it was to this that each newcomer hitched his horse. Then, with another glance around them, the trio moved across the plaza towards the bank. The hard eyes, glinting evilly in the deep shadow of hat brims, did not linger on the open door of the cantina. Probably the men were unable to peer out of bright sunlight into shaded gloom and see individual shapes.

The men entered the bank in single file and closed the door behind them.

'Got no chance with those guys,' Houghton said sourly. 'Rifle and two sixguns apiece.'

He was about to turn around to face the table again when another movement out on the plaza captured his attention.

16

Then he shrugged as he recognised the fat, moon-faced black-smith scuttling around the statue and lumbering towards the cantina, weighed down under an armful of horseshoes. The Pinkerton man was now completely out of range of sales talk, as he read avidly from a small, red-covered notebook.

'Trouble, señors,' the blacksmith announced breathlessly as he entered the cantina and shot a frightened glance over his shoulder. 'I smell it, with my nose.' He approached the table where the two men were sitting and set down the eight shoes in front of the drummer. 'You pay me now, señor.' It was not a question, but he added: 'Please.'

'Why trouble, Pedro?' Manuel called in English as the drummer began to examine the horseshoes like they were intricate pieces of machinery.

'You know I have the nose,' Pedro answered, wiping sweat from his forehead and leaving a dirt streak there. 'Those three.' He jerked a thumb over his shoulder towards the door. 'They don't smell good.'

The Pinkerton man finished referring to his notebook and snapped it closed with a nod. He stood up.

'What about the gun, sir?' Houghton pleaded and there was a tremor of desperation in his voice now.

Watching him, Steele decided the drummer's purchase of the shoes depended upon him making the gun sale.

'Don't bother me when I'm working,' the detective snarled.

Long moments of silence stretched out from the cantina to cloak the whole of Nuevo Rio. They created an ominous expectancy. Then one of the newcomer's horses stamped on the iron hard ground. A man screamed, another cursed and a shot cracked. The three sounds came from the bank. Then the door burst open and the men strolled out.

Pedro dived to the floor as Manuel ducked down behind the bar, dragging his wife with him. Steele snatched up his rifle but made no other move. Houghton swung around in his chair with his expression of concerned self-interest frozen.

'Stay quiet,' the Pinkerton man whispered, drawing his Remington.

The trio had emerged from the bank with careful slowness. Two of them raked their eyes and rifle barrels around the plaza.

The third, who was between them, carried a paper sack in one hand. He held his rifle low down, pointed negligently towards the open doorway of the cantina.

'Two guns gives you a better chance against three,' Houghton urged hoarsely.

The Pinkerton man gave a sigh of resignation which was at odds with his tense expression. Then, as he started towards the doorway, he scooped up Houghton's gun with his free hand.

'It's a good gun,' the drummer promised in a low whisper with a smile that looked sick.

'I'll let you know,' the Pinkerton man said.

Outside, the trio of bank robbers had reached their horses at the centre of the plaza. Their actions were quicker now, as they gained confidence from the lack of resistance. The Pinkerton man halted, still veiled by the shadowed interior of the cantina. The gun salesman slid smoothly off his chair and crawled out of the line of fire from the doorway. Steele eased back the hammer on his rifle. He saw the detective's neck flex into rigidity at the tiny metallic click. But the snorting of the horses as they were mounted was much louder.

Two long strides took the Pinkerton man into the doorway. He thrust both guns out in front of him. His tone was sharp, authoritative.

'Freeze it right there!'

Steele heard Manuel begin to whisper in rapid Spanish. The foreign words had the quality of a prayer.

'Briggs!' the man with the sack of money exclaimed.

The other two were reaching forward to unhitch their reins from the stucco sword handle.

'Drop the rifles!' the Pinkerton detective ordered. He was standing as stock still as the beheaded military governor.

Two of the men complied with the demand. As their rifles clattered to the hard ground they straightened in their saddles and clawed their hands into the air. The man with the sack of money half turned away from the detective, as if he intended to ignore him. The brief interlude of silence was even more intense this time. Even the horses respected it. The third rifle began to fall: but the sound as it hit the ground was swamped by a sudden shot.

18

The paper sack exploded and peso bills scattered. The horses reared and the Remington was wrenched out of Briggs' hand. It spun through the sunlit air, glinting. Then bounced to the ground. Dust coated the oiled surface of its buckled barrel. But while the gun was still in mid-air, Briggs put Houghton's product to the test. He fired through the shower of money and billow of rising dust erupted from beneath the stamping hooves of the horses.

Blasting the detective's gun from his hand had been pure luck. Now the man's good fortune ran out as his horse reared and he had to use both hands to hold himself in the saddle. The new gun exploded with a vicious crack and pulled violently to the right. The man took the bullet high in the shoulder and was thrown backwards, pitching head-first down the back of his canting horse. The animal gave a powerful toss of its head and snapped the model sword hilt. The injured man smacked to the ground amid the scattered money as his freed, panic-stricken horse made a rearing turn. The animal's forehooves crashed down upon him, catching him in the stomach. He screamed once, in the instant before impact. Then the metal rimmed hooves burst through his flesh. His blood-dripping entrails spilled out through the ghastly wound. The horse bolted, scattering severed lengths of slimy gore from its pumping forelegs. Flies swarmed in for a feast on the gaping wound. And the two remaining bank robbers realised they were free of physical restraint.

'Stay!' Briggs yelled.

Perhaps the pointing gun would have held the men. But their horses were spooked by the ravenous drone of the countless flies swarming in to satisfy their blood lust. The animals lurched forward. Briggs squeezed the trigger of the new gun. The hammer sprang up. Then jammed. With the horses taking care of the escape unheeded, both bank robbers had the opportunity to draw and fire. Briggs' anger held him in the open, struggling with both hands to free the mechanism of the jammed gun. He was hit twice. Once in the chest, which started to spin him. Then in the face. The second shot halted his turn and threw him backwards into the cantina. Blood gushed from an ugly wound at the side of his nose and Pedro scuttled into a far corner with a moan of horror as some of the warm stickiness sprayed over him. Something flew out of Briggs' pocket and skittered across the floor. It was the same colour as the man's blood. It came to rest against Steele's left boot and he looked down and recognised the red covered notebook to which the detective had referred.

Like everybody else in the cantina, Steele listened to the diminishing sound of the galloping hoofbeats. When they had faded into the distance of the plateau from where the men had come, he stooped and picked up the book. Then he crossed to where its owner was sprawled, as unmoving as only a dead man can be. His sightless eyes still held a trace of the anger in which he had died. His left hand was still curled around the butt of the gun which had induced his rage. Steele closed the eyes but did not attempt to flick away the settling flies from the face wound. There were too many of them.

'He is dead, señor?' Pedro asked. Then: 'I know he is. I smell it.'

Steele looked up from where he was crouched. Manuel and his wife were standing behind the bar, clinging to each other. The blacksmith was also on his feet, but needed to lean against the wall to stay that way. The drummer was sitting on his haunches, hugging his knees and rocking back and forth as he gnawed at his knuckles. Horror was inscribed deeply into the flesh of all four faces. Steele eased the new gun out of its death grip and scaled it across the floor. It stopped within easy reach of Houghton, but the salesman made no attempt to touch it.

'You'll have to find another buyer,' Steele said.

'God in heaven,' the drummer gasped.

Steele straightened up and nudged the corpse with his rifle muzzle before turning to head back to the bar for his coat. 'I wouldn't count on any advance endorsement,' he said quietly.

Chapter Two

NUEVO RIO had a small population. But it was an honest one in a time of tragedy. Even Manuel's cousin from the livery stable made no attempt to pocket any of the money as he helped his fellow citizens to collect the scattered peso bills. In addition to him, there was Manuel and his wife, Pedro and his wife, two men from the store and the elderly sister of the banker. The banker himself was dead, shot in the head with a rifle at short range when he objected to foul language in front of his sister.

The ten-year-old son of the blacksmith was excused the unpleasant chore of picking up the money from around the putrefying corpse sprawled at the foot of the statue. Instead, he was ordered to ride his father's burro the four miles to the next village south, where there was a priest.

As the Mexicans shuffled and stopped around the base of the statue, Ira Houghton sat in his buggy and stared ahead in a daze of disillusionment. Steele leaned against the doorframe of the cantina and leafed through the Pinkerton man's notebook. It was a cheap one with a cardboard cover and rough textured, unlined pages. Ten of the pages had been filled with small, neat handwriting, done in ink. Each page was ruled across to divide it into two sections. At the head of each section was the name of a man with, below, a physical description. The sections were all concluded with the name of a town, county or territory and then a price. In some instances the first price had been scored out and another substituted. Occasionally there was more than one correction. The new price was always higher than the old. Five of the sections had been completely scored through by a thick, diagonal line.

The number five rang a bell in Steele's mind which was now completely devoid of all after-effects of his long drinking bout. He glanced out into the plaza and saw why the number was meaningful. The Remington with the buckled barrel lay in the dust with its notched grip uppermost. There were five notches. With a pensive frown on his face, Steele referred to the notebook again and found a description to match the man who now lay in ghastly mutilation at the centre of the plaza. He was listed as Jake Turner with a price on his head of one thousand dollars, the reward posted by the town of Endsville, Arizona Territory. Finding the listings for Turner's buddies was easy for there was a note referring to the Thornton brothers – Fred and Allan – with whom he always rode.

But he wouldn't be riding with them any more. He was out of his league anyway: the Thorntons were worth two-and-a-half thousand apiece.

'What a waste for so little, señor.'

Manuel's sad tones brought Steele out of his concentration upon Briggs' neat handwriting and precise facts. He looked up and beyond Manuel and his wife he could see that the community work was over. The citizens of Nuevo Rio were returning to their tragically interrupted siesta.

'One thousand six hundred pesos, señor,' Manuel said as Steele moved out of the doorway to allow the old couple to enter. 'A fortune to anybody who lives in Nuevo Rio. To most people in the whole of Mexico. But to such men as them . . . ? Not enough to buy them women and whiskey for a week.'

'Enough for one of them to die for,' Steele replied.

The woman went on into the cantina, moving in a wide half circle to avoid getting close to the dead detective.

'If only it was him, señor. But Jose Muro and the lawman, too. It is bad.' He shook his head, grief-stricken.

Steele slid the notebook into his shirt pocket. 'It's an ill-wind,' he said.

'Excuse, señor?'

'Talking aloud my thoughts,' Steele replied. 'Nobody'll have any objection if I take him out of town with me?'

He pointed a blunt forefinger towards the dead man at the centre of the plaza. Manuel looked at the corpse with revulsion, then turned a confused stare towards Steele. The expression on the pale face of the young American offered no answer.

Manuel shrugged. 'It would be considered a favour, señor. Such a man does not deserve a priest. And it would be hard to find somebody to give him the dignity of burial.'

Steele nodded in acknowledgement, then stepped out of the sparse shade of the cantina wall to cross the plaza to the livery stable. Inside, the ramshackle building smelled of horse droppings and bad cooking. Manuel's cousin was eating a black tortilla and another was burning on an ancient stove. He halted his meal reluctantly and led Steele's mount from a stall with ill-will. Steele decided the man's attitude had less to do with the recent violence than with the lost opportunity to overcharge for his services.

Steele checked over the bay gelding and his saddle and bedroll. The animal seemed underfed and his gear smelled musty from neglect. But in a town like Nuevo Rio he was unable to take exception to either condition.

'Thanks,' he told the disgruntled liveryman after he had saddled the gelding and tied on his gear.

'I did little, señor,' the man replied.

'I know,' Steele countered as he led the horse out into the sunlight.

The man spat on to the stove and the moisture sizzled into steam. Ira Houghton's buggy was out on the trail up to the plateau, rolling slowly and raising only a small dust cloud. Pedro was just emerging from the cantina, his arms loaded with the horseshoes which seemed to be weighing him down more heavily now. He halted and looked at the gelding pointedly for a few moments as Steele hitched the horse to the cantina rail.

'No,' he said at length. 'They would not fit.'

23

Steele smiled as he turned to Briggs' horse and began to untie the bedroll. 'You smell it, Pedro?'

The blacksmith did not enjoy the humour. 'I smell only death, señor,' he said balefully.

'That's nothing special,' Steele replied as he unfurled the blanket and carried it out to cover the corpse. 'Not in this climate after it's happened.'

Pedro remained where he was, sweating with the strain of holding the horseshoes. He watched silently as Steele rolled the body of Jake Turner in the blanket and then tied it into an elongated bundle. He left a length of spare rope at each end and used these to tie the body in place after he had slung it across the saddle of the spare horse.

'I have been smelling it for a long time, señor,' Pedro said at last, as Steele swung across his own saddle and took up the reins of Briggs' horse as he unhitched his own with the other.

'Since when this guy and his buddies rode into town?' Steele suggested.

Pedro shook his head, the expression on his fleshy face becoming more mournful. 'Longer than that, señor,' he said softly. 'I told everybody, but they would not listen. I have smelled it since you rode into Nuevo Rio, señor.'

Steele looked long and hard at the round, sad face of the blacksmith and sensed a tightening of the skin over his own features. 'You're an expert?' he demanded. And it was a demand, his voice harsh, the words forced out between narrowed lips.

Pedro flinched upright, despite the weight of the horseshoes. He seemed on the point of back-tracking, but forced himself to remain where he was. 'Please, señor,' he said softly, nervously. 'I am a simple man who studies other men. You are not alone in being what you are. Many Americanos have passed through Nuevo Rio since the war in your country ended. Men who killed because it was asked of them. If they gained a taste for killing, who is to blame.'

'Pedro!' It was his wife, calling to him from the doorway of the blacksmith shop. Anxiety was etched into her careworn features.

'She worries,' Pedro said and a flicker of a smile reduced the

24

bitterness of his sadness. 'But as I told you, señor. I am a' student of my fellow man. Where you go, death will never be far away. You will attract it like a magnet. But you will never – '

'Pedro!'

Steele was aware that his face was still pulled into an expression of checked anger. 'Never what?' His tone was the same, too.

Now Pedro did back off a pace and the beginnings of fear replaced the sad smile. 'I think you will never harm a man who means you no ill will, señor. Excuse, I am called to eat.'

He backed away another pace, then sidestepped so that he was able to retreat without coming close to Steele. For a long time, Steele remained motionless in the saddle and Manuel – who had overheard the exchange – looked out from a window of the cantina and thought that the expression in the American's eyes matched that of the Pinkerton man's before his lids were pulled down. A dead man's stare lit with a glint of frozen anger.

Then Steele sighed and dropped the reins of his own horse. He took the other set of reins in his teeth and delved into a pocket of his jacket which hung from the saddle horn. He withdrew a pair of black buck-skin gloves which he slid on to his hands with measured care, smoothing out all the wrinkles. Although his actions were deliberate there was also something automatic about them, as if he were donning the gloves from habit.

He flexed his fingers and took up the two sets of reins again. 'Adios, Manuel,' he called softly, and touched his heels to the flanks of the gelding.

As the animal clopped across and out of the plaza at a walk, the emaciated Mexican swallowed hard and felt new sweat break out on his forehead. There seemed no reasonable way in which the American could have known he was being watched. He had not turned to look, and Manuel had made no sound. Yet the American had known.

'He is a different man, Manuel,' his wife called sadly from across the other side of the cantina.

Manuel shook his head as he turned. 'No,' he replied in the same tone. 'Pedro is right. He is the man he was before. He drank to try to forget what he is. What has happened today . . . it made him accept his fate.'

'His fate is to – '

'I do not know,' Manuel interrupted quickly, looking across the horrifyingly still form of the detective. 'But whatever it is, I hope he never returns to Nuevo Rio.'

Chapter Three

Up on the plateau to the north of the town the trail which ran towards the border was no longer clearly defined. Spur trails veered off to the east and west, connecting with the scattered dirt farms of the peons out of sight beyond the sun-parched hills of white rock and grey, lifeless soil. These were marked by frequent use. But few Americans elected to take the border crossing towards Nuevos Rio. And even fewer Mexicans went north this way.

As Steele crested the lip of the high, barren tableland he reined in both horses and surveyed the terrain ahead of him. It rolled away from him in a series of rises and dips, smooth topped in some cases and jagged in others: like an ocean that had been instantly fossilised at the height of a wild storm. Outcrops of rock, eroded by a million years of Sierra Madre weather, could have been the grotesquely battered wrecks of ships. And on the northern horizon a range of hump-backed mountains were like a distant shore. The mirages of silvered pools shining through the heat shimmer emphasised the similarity to a petrified ocean. But, here and there, living things destroyed the image. Clumps of mesquite thrust their twisted branches towards the blemish-free sky. Taller, thicker, more majestic saguaro cactus plants grew elsewhere. As if in confirmation, a bobcat streaked across on the periphery of Steele's vision.

'It's got to be the straightest line between here and there,' Steele said to the patiently waiting gelding.

The horse responded immediately to the touch of his heels and tautening of the reins, turning its head towards the west of north and starting forward at an easy, energy-conserving walk. In that direction lay the only visible pass through the distant mountains: a small vee of blue sky bitten out of the long ridge, as if by some gigantic shovel.

The straightest line, but by no means a straight one. For across such a chaotic landscape only a bird could make such unveering progress. A man on horseback was forced to make wide detours around the barriers of sheer cliff faces and long declivities of loose rock and shale where a false step could mean a broken leg or more. And sometimes wide ravines barred the way, seemingly bottomless so darkly shadowed were they.

At such obstacles Steele studied the ground which for the most part was too hard-packed to retain traces of those who had moved out ahead of him. But a patient, intent search to the left and right inevitably produced a definite result. A hoofprint or wheel track, a burnt-out cigar butt or horse-droppings fast dried by the blazing sun.

He trusted all the signs, reasoning that the Thornton brothers would have made themselves familiar with their escape route before hitting the bank: and that Ira Houghton, as a travelling man, would not drive his buggy blindly across such inhospitable and dangerous country.

As the sun crawled along its downslide towards the western horizon, the heat it spread across the vast emptiness of the land seemed not to abate at all. Steele's shirt and pants were pasted to his body by sweat and beads of moisture trickled out from under his hat, coursed down his face and splashed from his jaw on to the scarf. He was conscious that the fresh sweat was reviving the muskiness of that which had been squeezed from his pores during his self-imprisonment within the fetid atmosphere of the cantina in Nuevo Rio. But he could not smell the odour of himself. For the same sun which beat so harshly upon him

28

was also working on the decomposing flesh of the wrapped corpse. And the evil sweetness of the cloying stench of the rotting dead masked every other scent emanating from man and animals.

Darkness descended abruptly. At one moment the sky was bright blue and the sun a blazing yellow. Then the sun became a deep crimson and the sky changed to grey. The moon showed as a puffy white ball. The heat shimmer evaporated. The sun plunged out of sight and the heavens were black, sprinkled with glinting stars competing with a bright silver moon and losing. The black line of the mountains ahead were suddenly closer. The shot was distant.

Both horses pricked up their ears and the one with the ghastly bundle lashed to its saddle gave a nervous whinny. Steele peered ahead, his ears straining for further sound and his dark eyes seeking a visible sign to pinpoint the precise source. But the silence beyond the sounds of his own progress stretched into infinity.

There could be a thousand reasons for the single shot in the night, he told himself. But only one was presented by his own certain knowledge of the situation ahead. Two frightened and frustrated bank robbers on the run and one dejected gun salesman isolated in a private world of self-pity and guilt. If fear and negligence towards danger had come together at the wrong moment . . .

Throughout the long, slow, hot ride Steele had forced his mind to become a blank, concerned that he should not dwell upon the assessment and prediction propounded by the blacksmith of Nuevo Rio. But the distant shot and his continued progress northwards thrust the Mexican's ominous words out of memory and into the present. He fought to reject them, and won. Pedro was an ignorant peasant living in the middle of nowhere. The kind of man susceptible to the dangers of irrational thoughts in an enclosed existence where the mind had to find some outlet from hardship which had no reason.

It was after midnight and the intense heat of the day had been replaced by bitter cold when Steele saw the glow of a fire. He wore the sheepskin jacket now, buttoned to the neck and with the collar turned up to brush the underside of his hat brim. His pleasantly featured face was the only area of his being exposed to the night air and it was pinched with cold. For a long time he had been regretting his decision to shave off the month-old stubble which would have provided some protection.

He saw the glow of the fire against the sheer sandstone face of a hundred foot high cliff that angled from the south-east to the north-west less than half-a-mile ahead of him. He was on a much lower ridge which sloped down into a broad gully. The gully floor ran level for a long way, then apparently inclined down to where the fire burned. This was the way Steele went. The gully was littered with loose rocks, embedded in soft sand. This sand quickly trickled back into the small craters left by hooves but did not completely refill them. So he was able to see the moon-shadowed indentations made by Houghton's buggy and horse mixed with the disturbed tracks left by the Thorntons' mounts. The sand served yet another purpose: muffling the slow hoofbeats of the horses.

Short of where the gully floor either fell away sharply or sloped gently, Steele reined in both animals to a halt and dismounted. A clump of sagebrush clinging to the shadowed wall of the gully provided a tethering point and Steele left the horses there, sliding the Colt Hartford from his saddle boot before moving forward on foot.

The fire was less than a hundred yards away now, but he could still see only its flickering, reflected light on the face of the cliff which blocked off the dip on the far side of where the gully ended. A glance over his shoulder warned him that he was at risk of skylining himself. So he moved into the shadowed area of the gully and dropped down on to all fours: then on to his belly as he neared the lip of the slope.

He smelled boiling coffee and heard the indistinct drone of slow, low-voiced conversation. The bottom of the dip came into his vision and he halted his snake-like progress. The fire of mesquite kindling and prepared timber blazed brightly at the foot of the cliff which was less than a hundred feet down a sharp slope at the top of which Steele lay. The Thorntons sat on the far side of the fire, leaning their backs against the sandstone. Blankets were draped over their shoulders and they drank their coffee from mugs grasped in both hands. Three horses were

30

ground hobbled to a heap of rocks some twenty feet to the left of the fire. Ira Houghton's buggy was parked on the opposite side, leaning sharply forward on snapped shafts. But it was not only the shafts which had been fed to the fire. The sign had been taken off the roof and the side panels of the buggy had been wrenched free. The drummer was in no position to complain about the destruction of his property. He was curled beside the buggy with his knees drawn up to his chest and his hands out of sight between thighs and torso. The downward slope seemed to be of thickly layered loose sand which had been drifted into an even deeper covering at the base. Houghton seemed to have twisted and rolled a great deal, burrowing a shallow, open grave for himself.

Steele decided the drummer had been shot in the stomach and left to die in slow agony.

The fire glow bathed the Thornton brothers with bright light, the flames licking high enough to carry the column of smoke above them. Thus, Steele could see the men's faces as clearly as when they had been in the plaza of Nuevo Rio. Both were just a little older than thirty and bore a strong family resemblance in their deep-set, dark eyes which were too close together. Both had prominent, almost Roman noses and the sucked in cheeks and blotched complexions of men who did not eat enough of the right food. Both had brown hair fringed at the forehead and styled into widening sideburns. From the descriptions in Briggs' notebook Steele knew that Fred was the older of the two – thirty-three to Allan's thirty-one. And an inch taller at six feet. He decided Fred had to be the one on the right, who was doing most of the talking.

It was still not possible to overhear what was being said for the formation of the basin had the effect of trapping sound within itself. Even the crackle of the burning wood was muted. Only the sharp report of a revolver shot had managed to penetrate the acoustic trap to be dissipated across the barren void of the high plateau.

Steele made a final survey of the campsite below him, checking that the buggy offered the only cover in the immediate area. But although it was the sole defensive position, it was easily reachable by the two men.

31

He dragged himself backwards far enough to be able to stand erect, then moved quickly to where the horses waited. The biting cold of the night air had served to diminish the evil odour given off by Jake Turner's rotting flesh. But as soon as Steele unwrapped the blanket from around the corpse the stench was almost overpowering. The black crusting of congealed blood covering the ghastly wound of Turner's caved-in stomach formed a background to a seething mass of writhing white maggots. Others gorged at the shoulder wound.

Steele turned away in revulsion and clutched at his throat with gloved hands. He felt the bile swell up and forced it back by an effort of will. Then he took a deep breath from the fresh, chill air and turned towards the corpse again. He stared down at the massed scavengers for long seconds, until he was sure he could accept them. Then, turning away regularly to suck in fresh air, he worked on the putrid corpse. The waxy flesh and dormant muscles beneath were well advanced towards total rigor mortis. But the way in which the body had been transported gave Steele a good start on what he intended. The torso was already fixed into a forward-leaning posture. So it was just a matter of bending the knees and raising the arms in front of the body. The most difficult and repulsive task was to lift Turner's remodelled corpse into the saddle of Briggs' horse. The animal, accustomed to carrying such an evil-smelling burden, stood utterly still in patient resignation.

Final adjustments to the degree of bend in the legs forced Turner's feet into the stirrups. And a length of Briggs' lariat rope lashed around each calf and tied to the cinch at both sides ensured they would not come loose. The arms were bent into the perfect position to allow the reins to be wound around both wrists. The dead man's head was held upright, supported on a neck of solidified flesh.

Steele stepped back to examine the results of his labour and decided it would serve its purpose. At short range, with the horse as unmoving as the rider, the deception was obvious. But in different conditions, viewed by men in a totally different frame of mind . . . it would do, Steele decided.

Leaving his own mount hitched to the sagebrush, he led the other horse along the gully. He whispered gibberish in the

animal's pricked ear, concentrating upon keeping his tone sooth-
ing, reassuring. He had to halt further back from the top of
the slope now, to avoid silhouetting the mounted corpse against
the skyline. He released his hold on the bridle and continued
to speak softly to the horse for several more moments. Then
he eased slowly away from it, back-treading to the shadowed
wall of the gully. He stooped and held the rifle in one hand
while he gathered up several small pieces of rock in the other.
Then he went down into a crouch and moved forward on his
haunches. Next, on to his stomach, and dragged himself along
with his elbows, denting the loose sand.

There was a change in the basin. The fire was burning more
fiercely as the flames leapt up from fresh timber ripped from
the buggy. The coffee pot had been taken off and rested to one
side. The Thornton brothers were stretched out full-length
between the fire and the base of the cliff, lying close together so
that they could share the double thickness of each other's blankets. The blankets rose and fell with the rhythmic cadence of
sleep's regular breathing.

Where the gully ended at the top of the slope the walls were
crumbled into rock piles which were too low to throw more
than a token of moon shadow. So Steele stayed down and
merely rolled over on to his back, retaining his grip on the
rifle with one hand. He looked along the length of his body and
into the gully where the horse and its awesomely-still rider
stood. He lobbed one of the small rocks. The throw had the
height and length but was wide. It thudded softly into the sand.
The horse reacted to the sound with an indifferent turn of its
head. A second rock was also wide of the target, and longer
than the first. The animal turned its head more sharply and
took a tentative half-pace forward.

Steele gave a grunt – of satisfaction rather than irritation.
Although his aim was off, the sounds of the rocks landing were
having the effect of making the horse nervous. He purposely
aimed long with the third rock, sailing it just clear of the
corpse's hatless head to hit the sand two yards behind the horse.
The animal emitted a low snort and gave a skittish little jump.
Jake Turner swayed stiffly in the saddle. Steele lobbed the
remaining three rocks all at once. One went low and hit the

waxy face of the corpse, then bounced down on to the horse's neck. The other two found their mark on the animal's back. The spooked horse gave a loud snort of fear, reared and lurched into a panicked bolt.

Steele flung himself over on to his stomach and snatched the rifle into a firing position. The horse galloped level with him, showering him with sand from beneath the pumping hooves. Then it plunged down the abrupt incline, struggling desperately to stay four-footed as it slid over the treacherous, loose surface. The Thorntons were already sitting upright and flinging off their blankets by the time Steele had them in sight. And they had sprung fluidly to their feet and drawn their paired revolvers when the dead rider was carried into view and plunged down the slope on a cascade of disturbed sand.

'Don't shoot, Fred!' Steele bellowed at the top of his voice, confident that the precise direction from which the words came and any strangeness in the tone would not be discernible amid the confusion of sounds made by the headlong slide of the horse.

But a shot cracked as he spoke the first word. Steele saw the muzzle flash from one of the guns gripped by the taller man. Then heard the thud as the bullet impacted into dead flesh.

'It's Jake!' Allan Thornton shrieked.

He used one of his guns to chop down on one of his brother's arms and the two men stared at each other for long moments. With the source of its fear behind it, the horse had only one means of escape from the gully. Then all its animal instincts for self-preservation were concentrated upon keeping its footing during the breakneck slide. At the bottom, fire was an enemy. But then the scent of its own kind entered the animal's nostrils and it veered to the left.

Steele had planned for just such a reaction from the horse and a tight grin of satisfaction split his lips as he saw the animal lean into a turn and slacken pace towards the three hobbled mounts. Both the Thorntons were also watching the animal, their mouths pulled wide and their eyes bulging with shock.

'It can't be!' Fred Thornton yelled. 'We saw him with his – '

He snapped his head around to peer up the sand slope towards the gully mouth. His body stooped into a tense crouch and the muzzles of both his guns swung to follow his gaze. His brother was only a moment behind him in imitating his actions. But there was nothing to see except a shallow gap in the hill crest, brightly lit by moonglow. To the brothers' left of this gap there was a scattering of deeply shadowed rocks which had always been there as far as they knew. The fact that one of these shadows was Steele, frozen into immobility after lunging from the gully, could not be known to the tense watchers. Steele was in a crouch, the rifle with its metal parts between his body and the Thorntons. His head was slightly turned so that just his left eye was exposed, peering down the slope from between his upturned collar and pulled down hat brim.

The brothers were talking again, but in the low tones of before. Their voices were mere scratches on the silence but from the rigid postures of their bodies he knew that fear still retained a tight grip upon them. He was unable to see the horse with its dead rider, but none of the animals were making any noise. He breathed shallowly, but did not dare to move more than this. The seconds stretched interminably and his muscles began to ache. He told himself the pain was in his mind: that he had not held the rigid position long enough to invite cramp. But, despite the biting edge on the night air, he sweated. The moisture dried instantly and he smelled himself.

Then Allan Thornton moved, striding out of Steele's restricted range of vision: going towards where the horses were hobbled. The elder brother continued to aim his guns towards the mouth of the gully. Steele was too far away to see, but he could guess the man's eyes were raking back and forth along the entire length of the hill crest.

'Jesus Christ Almighty!' Allan roared. Then he choked and there was the ugly splashing sound of liquid vomit.

Fred whirled towards his brother and Steele lunged into abrupt movement again, diving forward along the brow of the hill. He covered only the length of his own body before freezing once more, head screwed around further to look down upon the whole basin. Allan had dropped to all fours beside the now quiet horse with its rigidly upright rider. He was being violently sick. Fred was running towards him. Steele snaked over some more ground, but this time angled down the slope instead of

35

along beneath the top. Fred reached his brother and became rooted to the spot as he saw the stage of crawling decomposition reached by Jake Turner's body.

But not for long. His reaction was practical instead of emotional. He yelled at his brother to get up. And when Allan did not respond, he grabbed him by his coat collar and yanked him to his feet. He leaned his own face close to the ghastly wanness of Allan's and bellowed at him.

'Saddle the horses, you bastard! Saddle 'em. I'll cover you.' He whirled away, releasing his brother and bringing up his guns. 'We gotta move. It's a stinking trick!'

Steele was three-quarters of the way down the slope and he froze again, pressing himself hard against the sand. The grit was sucked up his nostrils and dropped into his throat. He saw the elder Thornton stare directly at him, then look away again. So anxious to find an enemy he failed to spot him. But Steele silently chided himself for a fool instead of Fred Thornton. Why hadn't he left the brothers soundly asleep and taken the silent approach? Directly down the slope or in a half circle to steal up on them from the side? That would have been simple. Easy and safe.

Allan was beginning to carry out his brother's order. Lifting each saddle and throwing it across the back of a horse. But he was not working fast enough for Fred, who whirled and stooped to attend to fastening his own cinch. Steele risked a crouching running over the final few yards. He raised himself and loped down the last of the incline. Two more paces on the flat took him behind the vandalised buggy. He sucked in a deep breath and spat out the grit from his mouth.

Safe. That was the factor which had decided his approach to the capture of the Thorntons. He would have been safe. But what about them? They were outlaws, experienced in the shallow sleep of the guilty conscience. Able to wake to instant awareness and always ready to face the worst. They would have reached for their guns and Steele would have been forced to kill them. That was the chance he would have had to take. And it was a risk he was not prepared to accept – because of the crazy ramblings of an ignorant Mexican blacksmith who confused body odour with the smell of death.

'What about Jake?' Allan Thornton asked.

'What'd he ever do for us that earned him a burial?' Fred snarled in response.

The brothers were approaching the far side of the fire, leading their horses. Steele crouched low behind the wheel and still complete side panel of the buggy. They came into sight between the fire and cliff face. The elder brother constantly glanced up the slope, but with less conviction that there was somebody up there now.

'Some Mexican's idea of a lousy joke,' the elder man rasped, and holstered both his guns. 'If they was goin' to hit us, they'd a' done it by now.'

Allan had already slid his two sixguns into their tied down holsters. Both men stooped to gather up their blankets.

'Some joke!' Allan growled.

Steele stepped out from behind the buggy. They didn't hear him and he levelled the Colt Hartford. 'Real stinker, wasn't it,' he said.

Chapter Four

THE Thornton brothers were now awake and able to think before they acted. Their heads snapped up. Dark eyes, so recently recovered from one shock, bulged in the face of another. They saw the gun, then the cold-pinched face of the man holding it. The gun was trained on a point between their two bodies and the casual expression on the face did not suggest he was prepared to shoot. But neither brother was ready to risk his life on such a fleeting first impression.

'Who the hell are you?' Fred demanded.

Up close he looked older than specified in the notebook of the Pinkerton detective. But only because of a livid knife-scar that curved down from the corner of his left eye to the point of his jaw. At this moment, his brother seemed a lot younger. He was still very pale beneath a long day's growth of stubble and the gun frightened him. He lacked the self-assurance of Fred and seemed vulnerable.

'Somebody looking for something,' Steele replied.

'What?'

Allan dragged his eyes away from the menace of the gun muzzle and looked nervously at Fred. Steele guessed he was the kind of younger brother who had to be told what to do all the time: and was constantly afraid of doing it wrong.

'Money.'

Fred laughed. The sound was harsh, and so was the expression that accompanied it. His teeth were brown from tobacco smoke and black with decay. They were pointed, like the teeth of an animal of prey.

'Did you pick the wrong guys to stick up!'

'Don't undersell yourself,' Steele told him. 'You're a good investment. Five thousand dollars the pair.'

The difference between Fred Thornson's laugh and his snarl was small. When he snarled, the lips curled back a little more and the evil which lurked in his eyes was emphasised.

'So that's it! A goddamn bounty hunter!' He spat at the ground between himself and Steele. 'You enjoy making a living that way, mister?'

'Maybe,' Steele replied. 'It's my first day on the job. Ease the guns out nice and slow. And toss them over to the cliff.'

'And if we don't?' Fred challenged.

Steele continued to watch both brothers carefully. But he made his pose as casual as his expression, thrusting out a hip to lean against the buggy wheel. His tone was reflective. 'Whatever happened to a guy named Jake Turner?' he said.

Allan sucked in a noisy breath. Fred's attitude of defiance suffered a setback at the reminder. But he still looked mean and as taut as a coiled spring. 'We ain't wanted dead or alive, mister,' he rasped.

'Everyone makes mistakes the first day on a new job,' Steele replied.

'Where d'you plan on taking us?' Fred asked after a short pause during which he appeared to be wondering whether Steele was bluffing or not. He decided that the levelled rifle was more important than the casual attitude of the man holding it. His face relaxed into the lines of an indifferent expression of his own.

'Reward was posted in Endsville,' Steele replied.

Fred displayed a grin of pure pleasure which was incongruous under the circumstances. It worried Steele for a moment and he straightened up. Allan still looked as scared as before.

'Nice gaol,' Fred said easily. 'How was that with the guns again?'

'Slow,' Steele answered. 'Better make it one man at a time and one gun at a time. You first.'

'Fred?' Allan blurted anxiously.

'Do like he says, kid,' Fred answered, easing out the gun from the holster on his right hip, holding the butt delicately between his thumb and forefinger. He held it aloft for a moment, like something which disgusted him. Then he threw it towards the cliff. It hit the rock and bounced to the ground.

The two saddled horses scraped at the sand and pricked their ears. Fred, a faint smile still touching his lips, drew the second gun in the same manner as the first and tossed it away. Then he nodded to his brother, who mixed disappointment with his fear now. He had been expecting Fred to do something positive. But Fred continued with his passive compliance, stepping back a pace to allow Allan a clear aim at the cliff. The younger brother hesitated.

'Follow good examples and you'll live longer,' Steele urged.

'I ever let you down, kid?' Fred asked urgently and there was genuine concern in his voice and face.

Allan thought about it some more, then did what Steele had ordered. He drew each gun slowly, but anger sped the matched Colts towards the cliff face. The horses snorted. 'Now what?' the younger brother snapped petulantly.

'Rope hitched to your saddle,' Steele replied. 'Tie big brother's hands behind his back. Tight.'

'Like hell!' Allan snarled. 'You want it done, you do it!'

Steele sighed and swung the rifle a few inches, across and up. So that the muzzle menaced Fred's heart. 'Killing him might cost me two-and-a-half-thousand, but a man's got to be prepared to take the rough with the smooth.'

'For Christsake!' Fred yelled, whirling to put his back towards his brother and clenching his hands together at the base of his spine. 'This guy ain't all talk, kid.'

'But, Fred – '

'Do it!' his brother yelled.

Allan flinched, as if the words had a tangible force. Then he snatched the lariat from his saddle and uncoiled one end, moving in close to his brother. Steele watched carefully, making sure the rope was lashed tight around the wrists and that Allan did not use a slip-knot.

'Good enough for you?' the younger brother sneered as he stepped back.

'I want you to know I'm grateful to you,' Steele answered with a nod of satisfaction.

Then he lunged at Allan. At one moment he was leaning easily against the buggy wheel, apparently totally relaxed. The next he was thrusting forward, jerking the rifle out ahead of him in a bayoneting action. The fluid suddenness of the attack completely surprised the younger Thornton brother. He staggered back and thudded into his horse. At the same time, he jerked up his hands to grab for the rifle barrel. But Steele canted the gun and it smashed in below Allan's defence. The muzzle dug viciously into the man's groin and he screamed. High and thin. He grabbed for himself with clawed hands. Steele leaned to the side and turned his body. His gloved hands slid into a different grip on the rifle and swung it into a steeper tilt, bringing up the stock with a whip action. The fast rising stock connected with Allan Thornton's rapidly descending head. The impact was at the precise centre of the forehead and the injured man's scream was abruptly curtailed. He slumped to the sand, in much the same curled-up posture as the dead drummer.

Steele straightened and looked with indifference into the hatred-filled eyes of Fred Thornton. 'I'd 'a made him stand still for you, you bastard!' he roared.

'Like to do things my own way,' Steele answered softly, squatting down beside the unconscious man. He gestured with the gun and Fred backed off. The rope played out from the coil. Steele rested his rifle on the sand and drew the knife from out of his gaping pants leg. He cut the sliding noose from the rope and rolled Allan over on to his stomach. Then he tied the man's hands behind his back. The two brothers were joined together by the rope for a few moments, before Steele cut it.

Perplexity blunted Fred Thornton's slow burning hatred as he watched Steele tie the loose end of the rope into another noose.

'What the hell!' he snarled as Steele lifted Allan's head and slid the noose around his neck.

Blood from the burst flesh had formed a wide stain on the sand. It looked black in the flickering firelight. Steele stood up and moved over to the buggy to lean his rifle against it. The blade of the knife was bright silver splashed with red of reflected flames. He measured off about ten feet of rope, cut it and formed another noose.

'You going to stand still for me?' he asked.

Fred Thornton was an expert spitter. The range was long but the globule of moisture splashed on target between Steele's boots. Steele's expression did not change as he moved the knife back and forth in a beckoning gesture. Thornton stood his ground for a moment, then ambled forward and remained motionless as the noose was dropped over his neck. The knot was slid up under his left ear.

Steele tied the remainder of the lariat to the centre of the length which linked the two brothers together. Then he retreated to the buggy, holding on to the loose end of the rope. He pushed the knife back into the boot sheath and picked up his rifle.

'Where is Endsville?' he asked lightly.

Thornton stared at him in amazement. 'You don't know?'

'I'm from the East,' Steele replied. 'Stranger here.'

'Well, I ain't gonna tell you,' Thornton rasped.

Steele shrugged. 'I'll be the one riding easy while we look for it,' he said, and knotted the end of the rope to the buggy wheel. He moved towards the slope.

'You gonna leave us here like this?' Thornton called after him and for the first time there was a note of fear in his voice.

'Couple of minutes,' Steele shouted back as he started up the slope, his boots sinking deep into the loose sand. 'If you can wake up your brother we can make an early start.'

As he climbed the treacherous incline he glanced towards the far side of the fire and saw that Briggs' horse was still standing quietly beside that of Houghton. The dead Jake Turner continued to hold his rigid pose in the saddle. His own mount waited in the gully. He unhitched the reins from the sagebrush and swung into the saddle. He halted at the lip of the slope and watched Fred Thornton for a moment. The fire was low now, in need of fresh fuel. But it threw out enough light to illuminate

42

the whole basin still. And show the elder brother on his knees at the buggy, trying to unfasten the knot on the wheel with his teeth.

Steele urged the gelding forward and the animal started down the slope tentatively. He snorted his distrust of the surface as a foreleg sank deep into the sand. The sound caused Thornton to struggle to his feet, glowering with rage. Steele murmured softly to his horse and gave the animal his head, allowing him to choose his own course and pace. The gelding chose a diagonal line, crouching back to avoid a slide. Steele leaned the same way as his horse, helping him to stay balanced. They made the foot of the slope without toppling.

Allan Thornton was groaning as he returned to awareness and felt the pain.

'Couple of minutes wasn't nearly long enough,' Steele told Fred.

'Bastard!' the captive retorted.

Steele leaned down to gather up the reins of the brothers' horses and led the animals to the buggy. He hitched them to the wheel. 'Another two minutes,' he said. 'You're both either mounted or not. Maybe a mixture. Any way it is, I'm moving out. Hauling on the rope.'

He wheeled the gelding and walked him to the other side of the campsite. First he took up the reins of Briggs' horse from the stiff, icy-cold fingers of the dead man. Then he released Houghton's animal and yelled as he landed a sharp blow on the broad back. The horse whinnied and tossed his head. Then lunged into a gallop along the foot of the cliff. Steele watched him until he was out of sight among some boulders from an ancient rock fall. Then he waited for the dust to settle before leading the horse and dead rider back to the other side of the fire, which was now just a heap of dull red embers.

Both Thorntons were mounted, the linking rope drooping in a slack curve between them. Allan was slumped low in the saddle, his head lolling forward with his chin resting on his chest. Fred was eyeing him nervously, but turned to glower at Steele as he rode his horse around the buggy and leaned down to untie the two sets of reins and the rope.

43

'If he falls off we could both break our goddamn necks!' he rasped.

'Everyone has problems,' Steele replied, allowing the reins to fall and then hitching the rope to his saddle horn. 'Yours could be eased a little if I didn't have to wander all over the country trying to find Endsville.'

He eyed Fred quizzically and for several moments the prisoner pressed his lips firmly together. Then he gave a jerk of his head, not strongly enough to take up all the slack in the rope. 'Follow the cliff until you find a narrow canyon entrance. It cuts through this bluff. At the far end it's easy riding across open country into the foothills of the north range. There are plenty of ways up to the pass. Endsville's on the other side. Just over the border from Mexico.'

'I'm grateful to you,' Steele said.

'Don't be,' Fred snarled. He turned to look at his brother. 'That kind of gratitude I can do without.'

'It was better than killing him with kindness,' Steele answered and heeled his horse forward.

'Stay with it, kid,' Fred urged anxiously. 'The bastard's moving us out.'

The reins on Briggs' horse were shorter than the rope. The animal moved forward obediently in the wake of the gelding.

'Now!' Fred exclaimed loudly and Steele whipped around in the saddle.

But it was not a call to attack. Both brothers dug in their heels simultaneously and their horses started in the wake of the lead pair. The group had to make a turn to go in the direction Fred Thornton had indicated. Steele steered the gelding into a wide sweep and the trailing horses followed the precise line. The ropes linking the brothers together and to Steele remained slack. They circled the derelict buggy, the dead Ira Houghton and the dying fire. Then followed the tracks of the freed horse.

'Jesus, mister, why don't you ditch Jake,' Allan groaned. 'He don't smell good.'

His teeth began to chatter, but not from abstract fear of the dead. Away from the fire, the night air bit through the brothers' sleeveless waistcoats and thin shirts. They had left their hats back at the campsite along with the blankets.

44

'A thousand and one reasons,' Steele replied. 'The odd one is that I don't believe you three aren't wanted dead or alive. Which makes the other thousand obvious.'

'So why didn't you just blast me and the kid if you know that?' Fred demanded. 'Ain't no other bounty hunter I've heard of would have done it the hard way.'

'I'm a special kind,' Steele answered.

'The stupid kind!' Fred snapped out, the cold affecting his voice, giving it a tremor. 'Like that clown Briggs. Got himself a rep for bringing 'em in alive. Since you picked up what was left of Jake you must have seen what happened to Briggs.'

Apart from his discomfort at the cold, the elder Thornton seemed at ease again. His mood the same as it had been when Steele announced he intended to take his captives to Endsville.

'There when it happened,' Steele said. 'Grandstand view from the cantina in Nuevo Rio.'

'Briggs always worked alone,' Fred said quickly, his tone implying that he considered Steele a liar. 'We ought to know. He's been on our trail for long enough.' He gave a short laugh. 'Well, he *was* on our trail.'

'You had a lucky break,' Steele accused. 'Then killed the man who gave it to you.'

'The drummer?' He made the word sound like an obscenity. 'What'd he do for me and the kid?'

'It was one of his guns that jammed up on Briggs,' Steele replied as he steered the gelding into the mouth of the narrow canyon.

Fred concentrated upon maintaining the same degree of slackness in the ropes as the sharp turn was made. Allan was still in pain from the jab in the groin and smack on the head but the bitter cold had hastened the clearing of his mind. He was fully aware of the circumstances now and able to synchronise his actions with those of his brother without any urging from Fred.

'Just luck,' Fred said off-handedly when all the horses were moving on a straight course again, between the high, rugged walls of the canyon. 'Good for me and the kid. But he got some bad when he drove out of the end of that gully and came skidding down that sand slope. Guess the stupid bastard didn't see the way the land fell away. The kid and me was just setting up camp. You know what happened back in that Mex village. Only natural that the kid and me didn't just stand there waiting for the guy to step outa his buggy. Goddamn buggy was coming down that slope straight at us. So we blasted at it. Got him twice in the gut.'

'And you just left him to die.'

'Didn't take but twenty . . . thirty minutes,' Fred replied evenly. 'We lit a fire for him.' The familiar short, harsh laugh. 'You know, when he saw those flames he likely figured he was in hell already. He sure screamed like he did. Ain't that right, kid?'

He laughed again, and his brother giggled. The evil sound echoed between the high walls. Steele listened to the actual laughter, the echo and then the memory of it inside his mind. He tried to use it as a foundation upon which to build up hatred against the two killers he had at his mercy. But he couldn't raise it above the level of thought about the four men who had died so uselessly: and whose deaths had left not the slightest impression upon the Thorntons. For was he not as one with the brothers? He had killed. In the war, but that could be discounted. In the violent peace that followed it, though. Tracking down the men who lynched his father and making them pay. Killing others, too, who stood in his way. And finally murdering Jim Bishop, his best friend. But Bish was also a lawman whose duty it was to make Steele pay for breaking the law.

There had been hatred enough then. The degree of hatred he had to generate to kill. And he had dug too deeply: exhausted his reserve. There was none left.

He rode out of the gloomy canyon into the brightness of a moonlit wilderness stretching in shallow folds of featureless hills towards the mountains.

He decided that his long retreat into the slough of drunkenness had not been wasted. For he had ridden into Nuevo Rio as a man confused and lost, his emotional stability shattered. And he had emerged from the long drunk and the primitive town as a new kind of man. It would take time to discover every facet of what he had become. But each new experience revealed another piece of the jig-saw.

He still had the ability to show kindness. His dealings with Manuel at the cantina had witnessed that. And to control his anger: Pedro had been allowed to return to his anxious wife while Steele withheld his ire. He could stand by and watch men die, without flinching or involving himself until it suited his purpose – as in the aftermath of the bank robbery. And he was able to work coldly and relentlessly to achieve what he wanted.

All this, he accepted. With no sense of pride or surge of pleasure. Certainly no shame that some of his instincts matched those of the Thornton brothers. What concerned him as he rode through the canyon was his inability to hate, which blocked his well-practised aptitude to kill. But, as he rode clear of the high walls and angled across the open country towards the mountain pass, he accepted this, too. For he recognised it as a safety factor in his new character. And as something that cancelled out all traits he might share with the Thorntons and men like them.

He was not a cold, calculating killer, despite the war and that violent peace before Nuevo Rio. And neither was he allowing his actions to be dictated by the ominous warning of the fat blacksmith. If he ever killed again the act would have to be inspired by one of two things. Hatred, should the seeds be implanted. Or self-preservation. And in the present circumstances he had neither motive.

'He's quiet, ain't he, kid?' Fred said to end a long period of silence marred only by the clop of hooves and creak of leather.

'Worrying about whether he's doing the right thing, maybe, Fred,' Allan replied.

'Like he told me a while back, everybody's got problems,' the elder Thornton countered.

Both men were endeavouring to inject a taunting note into their voices. But the intense cold that was reaching deep into their flesh to chill their bones muffled the bite in the words.

'I've only got just the one,' Steele tossed over his shoulder.

'What's that?' Fred muttered, uncaring.

'Why in hell did I decide to be a bounty hunter,' Steele answered.

'You won't get no argument if you want to chuck it in right now,' Allan growled.

47

'Can't do that.'

'Why not?' Fred's tone was sour.

'I need the money.'

'There's easier ways of making it,' Fred answered.

Allan withdrew into his private world of pain numbed by cold, sure the talk would not lead to their captor releasing them.

'Like robbing banks?' Steele suggested, turning in the saddle to show the Thorntons a grim smile.

Fred spat, far to the side, aiming at a rock and hitting it. 'Jake was bored. He wanted some action. We don't usually work that way. We make plans.' He looked ruefully at the rigidly swaying form of the dead man taking the enforced ride ahead of him. 'Now he's seen the last action he'll ever make.'

Steele glanced fleetingly at the ghastly crater in the mortified flesh. 'No stomach for it any more,' he said.

Chapter Five

THE strange group rode into Endsville three hours after sun up, dropping down out of the high, barren pass into a broad hollow, sheltered and lush with green pastureland watered by several small streams rising among the surrounding rocks. The town was well named for it stood at the meeting point of three trails: from the north, east and west. It was comprised of three streets in the form of a large tee, flanked by a mixture of single and double storey frame buildings. Those lining the south side of the trails coming in from California in the west and New Mexico Territory in the east presented an almost solid barrier to the pass and Mexico beyond. Thus, the town quite literally was turning its back on the border.

Steele could not recall passing through Endsville on his headlong flight from the law and the past. And, as he led the horses and his prisoners down the grassy slope in the pleasantly warm sunshine of early morning, he realised that it was quite likely he had not done so. The American-Mexican frontier was a long one and he had been coming from the east. He could have crossed the Rio Grande from Texas or entered Mexico at any point west of El Paso. Perhaps been south of the border for days before riding into Nuevo Rio.

'Don't expect no brass band welcome, mister,' Fred Thornton called with a harsh laugh.

Steele glanced over his shoulder at the two brothers and both of them grinned happily at him. Their humour had been improving at the same rate as the sun's warmth. Previously, the intense cold of the high mountain air had held the men in a trap of silent self-pity, which was the way Steele wanted it. Despite their lack of weapons and the threat of broken necks should one brother make a move unmatched by the other, Steele did not trust the men's passive compliance. He felt sure that it was not in the nature of the Thorntons to surrender so easily without having an escape plan in mind. Which was why he had dictated the long ride through the bitter night instead of holding off beside the warmth of the camp fire until morning. He suffered from the cold, too, but his sheepskin jacket and hat kept out the worst. The Thorntons were dressed for the heat of the day and were minus their hats. Exposed to the severe cold and unable even to breathe on their bound hands, the brothers were in no condition to put up any kind of fight. Were probably too distressed to even think about anything but their misery.

But with the sunrise had come a change of mood. Fred seemed genuinely happy and this, allied with a confident recognition of Steele's reluctance to kill, led him to barrage his captor with a stream of taunts. His brother, still very pale except where a large patch of dark bruising and congealed blood spread over his forehead, entered into the spirit of the barbed humour, giggling on cue.

'You have friends down there?' Steele asked evenly.

'Wouldn't say that,' Fred replied and this erupted more childish sounds of amusement from his younger brother. 'Though there might be a couple.'

'Nah, Fred,' Allan said. 'They ain't in town yet.'

'Might have got in early,' Fred suggested.

Steele turned his back to the prisoners again, noting that Jake Turner's body was beginning to lose its rigidity – and to release the stench of decomposition – now that the deep freeze of the night was gone.

Endsville looked peaceful, facing up to the day at a calm,

measured pace. Smoke drifted lazily from many chimneys. Voices droned out of opened windows. A few people were abroad on the broad sidewalks. A buckboard approached town on the northern trail and two women rode in sedately from the east. About five hundred head of cattle grazed in scattered groups to the west. The only ranch in the broad basin stood just below the north-western rim, beyond the grazing herd. Two mounted cowhands rested in their saddles, smoking as they stood loose guard over the beef.

Steele was struck by the thought that it didn't look the kind of town two outlaws ought to be happy to be captured in. It seemed pleasant and law-abiding: not the sort of rip-roaring border town which offered law-breakers the safety of numbers.

He led his charge through a gap between two double storey buildings just short of where the street ended and became the open trail to the west. They were both private houses with neatly-tended, picket-fenced gardens at the front. The appetising aromas of boiling coffee and frying bacon drifted through the windows. The mixed scents of the clusters of flowers growing in the gardens combined with the cooking smells to cut across the stench of long dead flesh.

Steele was gripped by a poignant memory of summer mornings at the plantation house in Virginia.

'Sure hope we get to eat in the gaolhouse,' Fred's growling voice announced, cutting violently across Steele's thoughts.

Steele became aware of many pairs of watching eyes, but as he lowered his lids against the strong sunlight angling in over the eastern rim of the basin he could see nobody. Private houses continued to flank the street for two hundred feet and then came the business section clustered around the three-way junction. The people who had been on the sidewalks were no longer in sight. Two saddled horses were hitched to a rail, sucking water from a trough, but the women who had ridden them in were nowhere to be seen. The buckboard rattled slowly around the corner and slowed to a halt. The driver climbed down quickly and disappeared through a doorway. He did not look back along the street towards Steele and his prisoners. Not until he was within the safety of the building, anyway. Then, Steele guessed,

51

the man probably became another secret watcher. For he realised his mind was not playing tricks on him. His sense of being under surveillance was valid: nervous eyes were following the progress of the newcomers – from behind lace curtains and the shadowed interiors of the business premises. They watched in silence: the only sound to be heard in Endsville the clop of hooves from four horses. The town seemed to be holding its breath in the mild warmth of morning: frightened by the macabre appearance of the group and willing the men, with an almost physical urging, to ride on through.

They rode into the centre of town, Steele's pleasantly handsome features set in an expression of impassive indifference, with lips pursed and dark eyes directed negligently ahead. Behind him, the Thorntons looked alternately to the left and right, grinning incongruously above the menacing nooses held tight around their throats. Jake Turner's body drooped forward, the head lolling to each side, brushing the neck of Briggs' horse.

They rode between a church and a livery stable; a bank and a general store; an express office and a saloon; a blacksmith's and a feed and grain store. The sheriff's office and gaolhouse was on the south side of the main street, facing Endsville's second street which ran into the northern trail. Several stores, a restaurant, an hotel and a newspaper office made up the rest of the town's business centre.

As Steele turned his charges towards the front of the sheriff's office, Jake Turner's body toppled to the left and swung at the side of the horse, held to the saddle by the ropes around his feet and the stirrups.

'Jake don't look happy,' Fred Thornton growled.

'Reckon he wants to find a hole and crawl into it,' Allan countered. 'Get some sleep.'

Steele swung out of the saddle and hitched his own and Briggs' horse to the rail. Then he tied the rope in the same manner and stretched luxuriously, flexing muscles cramped from the long ride and made tauter by tension. The horses stood in obedient silence. Thus, the rattle of the opening door was amplified by the hushed atmosphere which gripped the town.

'You wanna see me?'

The speaker was framed in the doorway of the sheriff's office, wearing a star on his chest to proclaim his right to be there. He was about forty, with the smooth, unlined face and bulging belly of a man who has had an easy life. He had just a little black hair arched over each ear and a tiny curve of moustache above his pouting lips. He had no eyebrows and his soft brown eyes looked naked and vulnerable above his puffed cheeks. He injected meanness into his voice but his eyes were a truer reflection of his mood. He was apprehensive. He wore a gunbelt with shells slotted around it, but the single holster was empty. A trickle of grease on his chin indicated he had been having breakfast.

'Hi, Sheriff White,' Fred Thornton greeted easily. 'This is Sheriff White, mister. Guy didn't tell us his name, sheriff.'

The lawman ignored Thornton. Instead, he looked from Steele to the sagging figure of the dead man, then back at Steele again. He wrinkled his snub nose against the assault of the stench.

Steele nodded. 'If it was the law posted the rewards on these three.' He jerked a thumb. 'That one's Jake Turner, by the way. In case you don't recognise him from this angle.'

'Figured he was,' the lawman replied, not advancing across the threshold of the office. 'You kill him?'

'No. He took a bullet from a Pinkerton man and fell off his horse. His horse killed him. Bank raid over the border.'

White looked at the Thorntons. 'That right?'

'On the nose, sheriff,' Fred answered. 'Then we upped and blasted that detective. Me and the kid. Mex town. Out of your jurisdiction. This here bounty hunter got a tricky drop on us. I hear you got a nice clean gaol. Hope we ain't missed out on breakfast.'

White grimaced. 'Get 'em down and bring 'em in, mister,' he told Steele. 'Not the stiff. Mortician lives out at the end of North Street. He's got a place out back to keep the bodies until they're buried.'

'I've earned my money bringing in the wanted men, sheriff,' Steele said. 'Now you earn yours and let the undertaker work for his.'

White seemed about to argue the point but Steele's impassive expression, casual attitude and even tone carried a tacit warning which was more aggressive than a show of anger would have been. 'Zeke!' he yelled over his shoulder, then stepped out on to the sidewalk, blinking his naked eyes in the strong sunlight.

A thin, moon-faced kid of about eighteen emerged from the law office. He had obviously heard the exchange of conversation, but now got his first sight and smell of the putrefied body. 'Jesus,' he gasped.

'Don't blaspheme, boy,' White chided. 'Give me a hand to get the two live ones down. Then go get Marty Trotter and tell him to bring his hearse.'

Steele watched idly as the fat sheriff and skinny boy carefully eased the helpless Thorntons out of their saddles and set them on the ground between the horses. The two outlaws were as stiff as Steele but a lot weaker. As Zeke edged around the sagging body and then streaked away along North Street, and the sheriff unhitched the rope from the rail, the prisoners stood shoulder-to-shoulder, supporting each other. There was no humour in them now.

'Hard way to bring 'em in, mister,' the lawman growled as he loosened the running knots and lifted the nooses from around the Thorntons' necks. Thick bands of angry redness marked the men's flesh.

Steele indicated Turner. 'Harder for him. Lot quieter, though.'

White nodded for the Thorntons to step up on to the sidewalk and go into the office. They staggered and swayed, but made it. White crowded in behind them and Steele brought up the rear as a black bodied wagon rolled out on to North Street and started down towards the junction.

The office was neat and clean, spartanly furnished with a desk, three chairs, a file cabinet, couch and rifle rack. A closed door led out to a room at the back. There were just two cells, formed by a partition of steel bars down one side of the office. Both doors stood open. White made each brother stand facing into a cell. Then he used a paper-knife to saw through their bonds and gave the order to move inside. He clanged and locked both doors. The Thorntons sank gratefully on to their mattress-covered cots and massaged their chafed wrists.

The sheriff dropped into a swivel chair behind the desk. On the desk was a tray bearing the remains of a bacon and egg breakfast, along with a coffee pot and empty mug. He pulled open a drawer and took out a sheaf of wanted bills. Steele approached the desk, drawing Briggs' notebook from his pocket. He flipped it open and used the sheriff's pen to score through the sections devoted to the Thornton brothers and Turner.

'Six thousand, sheriff,' he said.

'I ain't gonna take your word for that,' White replied sourly.

'We're under-valued,' Fred Thornton called cheerfully. 'Only takes account of the trouble we caused in Endsville. You oughta run us in to El Paso, mister. Me and the kid's worth five grand apiece there.'

White looked up, hope on his round, overfed face. 'You wouldn't want to do that, mister?' A tepid smile flicked over his features. 'We'll pay you for the stiff.'

Steele nodded towards the cells. 'They've had a rough time. Now they look happy. Wouldn't want to spoil it for them.'

White sighed, not disappointed. The hope had been a faint one. He returned to flipping through the wanted posters, found what he wanted and did some mental arithmetic before giving a weary nod. 'Six grand is right. I don't keep that kind of money here. You'll have to wait until the bank opens.'

'Fine,' Steele said, dropping into one of the two chairs in front of the desk. He reached over and picked up the sheaf of bills.

White surrendered them without protest and watched quizzically as Steele ran through them. Then, the stockily built, grey haired bounty hunter began to copy some details into the red notebook. Descriptions of wanted men not already noted by Briggs: and only those who had more than a thousand dollars on their heads.

'That book belonged to the Pinkerton detective,' the lawman said after a long pause, interrupted every now and then by a plea from Fred Thornton about breakfast. His hunger was ignored.

'You know him?' Steele asked without looking up.

'He came through here on his way into Sonora,' White answered. 'Did just what you are, mister.'

Outside, Endsville had taken up its morning routine again. The body of Jake Turner had been freed from the horse and placed in a plain pine box. As it was carried away in the enclosed hearse, only the four travel weary horses hitched to the rail remained in sight as a reminder of the macabre visitors to town. Zeke entered the law office and moved quickly across it to disappear into the rear of the building. He looked as if he was going to be sick. He left the street door open and the sounds of the town going about its business drifted in.

'Weren't the Thorntons and Turner in town then?' Steele asked.

'Staying at the hotel,' White answered, unabashed. 'But Briggs didn't ask about them. Just asked about Dave Street and Arnie Duff. I ain't ever come across them.'

Street and Duff had entries in the notebook, made by Briggs himself. They were wanted in Laramie, for rewards of three thousand dollars each. The crime listed on the posters was murder. The wording on the bills naming the Thornton brothers was more specific: WANTED FOR THE MURDER OF ANNE SLAUGHTER. Turner was worth less, for his crime was merely being an accessory to the same killing.

The silence which followed his last remark seemed to irritate White. 'Ain't you gonna ask me why I let wanted men live in this town without arresting 'em?' he demanded.

Steele completed his notations and pushed the pile of bills across the desk. 'Why should I worry about that, sheriff?' he asked evenly as he slid the notebook into his pocket. 'If you had done your official duty, I'd still be broke.'

White looked long and hard into Steele's nonchalant eyes, searching for a tacit accusation of cowardice. He found none, but still felt the need to excuse himself. 'Anne Slaughter was nothing more or less than a whore. A disgrace to this town. But old man Slaughter was rich. Owned the North Ranch up on the long hill. The murder of the Slaughter woman was the first crime committed in this town for years. And it happened three years ago. Old man Slaughter posted the reward. Then he died. Of a broken heart, some'll tell you. I don't know and I don't give a damn. We got new people up at the North Ranch. And the town's been quiet and law-abiding again. We got no whores. And until you brought 'em in, we had no outlaws with mean friends locked up in our gaol.'

'You want me to apologise?' Steele asked, as the big hand on the wall clock clunked over a final segment to stand at nine o'clock.

'I want nothing from you,' White replied. 'I detest bounty hunters. You bring in the men, pick up what's owed you and drift outta town. It's me and others like me have to sit it out, sweating that the circuit judge gets here before the prisoners' friends.'

Steele raised himself slowly from the chair, his tired body protesting at the need to make a move. 'Be grateful if I could have my money now, sheriff,' he said softly.

'I won't say it's been nice meeting you, mister,' Fred Thornton called from where he was stretched out on the cot. 'But I'm sure looking forward to crossing your path again.'

He spat and the spittle arced through the shaft of sunlight penetrating a high window and splashed into a slops pail. Allan giggled.

'Pleasure will be mutual,' Steele replied as he headed for the door and the sheriff hauled himself up from behind the desk. 'Shall we say somewhere close to El Paso?'

'You won't ever get that lucky, bounty hunter,' the elder Thornton snarled.

Steele pursed his lips. 'I'll take my chances,' he challenged evenly.

'Let's go get your money, mister,' the fat sheriff urged.

'I'm as anxious to do that as you are,' Steele told him.

'Spend it fast, bounty hunter!' Fred Thornton yelled as Steele was hustled out of the office by White. 'Or could be your life will run out before your loot.'

Allan giggled.

'Why the hell didn't you blast 'em, mister,' the sheriff said with a sigh as they stepped down from the sidewalk and started across the street towards the Endsville Bank. 'Been easier for you, me and everybody concerned.'

'Sheriff?' Steele said softly.

White's head snapped around and saw again the quiet menace in the casual expression of the grey haired young man walking beside him. 'What?'

Steele tapped his own narrow chest and his tone was suddenly cold: as bitingly chill as the night just gone. 'I'm the only one who concerns me,' he said.

Chapter Six

SHERIFF WHITE did not hang around in the bank after he had authorised the diffident teller to pay Steele the six thousand dollars left in Slaughter's account under the old rancher's will. But when Steele emerged, enjoying the bulge of the bankroll in his pocket, he saw the lawman. Hurrying towards his office from the Border Restaurant, carrying a tray draped with a cloth. Steele guessed the tray held breakfast for the Thornton brothers.

When he saw Steele coming back across the street towards him, the sheriff stood hesitantly in the doorway of his office, his eyes filled with apprehension again. 'You have trouble of some sort, mister?' he asked.

Steele showed his quiet smile. 'They say money's the root of a lot of it, sheriff,' he replied. 'But mine hasn't started yet.'

He began to unhitch the gelding, aware once more that he was the subject of a secret surveillance. But not of the massed kind this time. The street was busy with traffic: horses, wagons and people. But rather than watching him, the citizens of Endsville and the surrounding area seemed to take great pains to avoid looking at him. As he swung up into the saddle, he looked to his left, along East Street. And saw the woman a moment before she ducked back into the doorway of *Benson's Guns and Ammo*

Store. She wasn't taking a first look at him. He had seen her leaning out of the doorway while the sheriff was accompanying him to the bank.

'Leaving town, like I said?' the fat lawman asked mournfully.

'Not for a while,' Steele replied, backing the gelding out from the clutch of horses. 'I need to catch up on some sleeping and bathing. Hotel any good?'

'Only one we got,' White answered, and seemed pleased that the bounty hunter intended to stay in Endsville. Was happy enough to supplement the information. 'The beds are changed regular and there's no vermin.'

'For what else could a man ask?' Steele acknowledged.

Sheriff White went into his office with a smile on his face as Steele walked the gelding down West Street to the livery. He paid in advance for feeding, watering and quartering for a day. The middle-aged owner accepted the instructions and money and then delegated the chores to a spotty-faced youngster not long out of school. Both the man and boy treated Steele with the kind of surly respect he realised he was going to have to get used to. For he knew that he now carried the indefinable mark of the killer. Nothing so clearly identifiable as the smell of death spoken of by Pedro. But something about his expression, the way he moved, spoke . . . that went beyond the sight of him leading the two prisoners and a corpse into Endsville. For the Thorntons were now in gaol and Turner's body was on its way to the final resting place. Yet it was his presence in the livery rather than the recollection of the grim tableau which affected the liveryman and the boy. Steele felt this strongly.

He meant neither of them any harm, and yet he could see the fear of him in their eyes. And they seemed to have to struggle to keep their lips taking the line of a grimace. Their attitude bothered Steele and as he went out of the livery he realised that it meant he was in no way at all like the man he used to be. Even when the death and violence was over, its evil clung to him like an invisible shroud: impressing upon normal people that he was not like them.

As he moved along the sidewalk, prepared to move to the side of those he approached, he found himself walking a precisely straight line. For it was others who veered away in hurried, fearful steps. He crossed North Street and moved along East, sweating profusely under the thick jacket with the collar still turned up. The Colt Hartford rifle was resting across his right shoulder, the inscribed stock plate glinting in the sunshine.

The woman who had been in the doorway of the gun shop was now standing behind the counter. There was apprehension in her eyes as Steele turned into the shop. But mixed with it was a subtle curiosity. Her greeting was bright and not forced.

'Good morning, sir.'

Her voice was as pretty as her face, which meant it was rather immature – girlishly coy. She was in her late twenties – an age when the mere prettiness of youth should have become the beauty of womanhood. But instead, her physical appearance seemed to have been arrested some years ago and her features had stayed elfin, with a certain mischievousness in her green eyes. She actively encouraged her childlike quality by wearing her long blonde hair in pigtails. But her dress, although it was simply and modestly cut, could not entirely mask her fully developed figure, thrusting and swelling beneath the gingham material.

But it was not only the fullness of her body which betrayed her true age. Rather, it was seen through the surface ingenuousness of her eyes: a wealth of experience was stored there and Steele was uncomfortably aware his masculinity was being closely examined by a sensuous woman of the world.

He replied to her greeting with a non-committal nod, and slid his hat from his head. 'Like some shells for this rifle, ma'am,' he said. 'They'd be forty-fours. I'll take six cartons.'

He held up the Colt Hartford for her to see.

'It's miss, sir,' she corrected. 'Miss Jessica Benson. Happy to serve you.'

Her petticoats crackled beneath the gingham dress as she walked to the far end of the counter. Her movements were graceful, very feminine. They comprised another pointer to her age and awareness of a man's eyes following her.

'Oh, and two cartons of forty-one calibre for an under-and-over,' Steele called.

'No trouble, sir,' Jessica replied, stretching up to a high shelf. Her posture was awkward for her, but designed to present her body in profile towards Steele – ensuring he could see the way the bodice of her dress stretched over her breasts.

As Steele looked at her and experienced a sexual stirring, he became aware of being watched himself. He snapped his head around – and was in time to see the abrupt sway of a drape curtain masking an archway behind the far end of the counter.

'You're not a lawman, sir?' Jessica posed as she moved back towards Steele, her long-fingered, well-kept hands loaded with cartons.

'No, miss.'

'Bounty hunter then?'

The curtain had stopped swaying now, but Steele could sense the presence of somebody lurking in the archway.

'Forgive me for being curious, sir,' the woman said when Steele did not reply immediately. Her smile was bright, interested. 'But we don't get many strangers in Endsville. And I can't ever recall any man that rode into town quite like you did.'

'Bounty hunter is right,' Steele told her, choosing to ignore whoever waited behind the curtain as he watched Jessica start to wrap the cartons of shells. 'Doesn't seem to be much to bring in strangers.'

She nodded and sighed. 'That is absolutely right. When they built the town it was called Borderville. The folks intended it to be the main crossing point into Mexico, what with the pass and the three trails meeting here.' She smiled wryly. 'But you came in over the pass from the south, didn't you, sir? Guess the folks who built this town didn't look to see what's on the other side of the mountains. Nothing, for an awful long way. Not many people want to cross here.'

'The basin looks pleasant enough, though,' Steele said.

Jessica sighed again as she looped string around the package. 'I guess so. The folks were pretty smart. Or just lucky maybe. There's the basin and a couple of valleys nearby that are good cattle and growing land. Unusual for this part of the territory. So we have some nice farms around Endsville. Folks do better than get by. But it's all pretty dull.' She looked up and smiled brightly. 'Would you mind, sir?'

She was in the process of knotting the string and needed Steele to put his finger on the tie. He did so, leaning across the counter. He smelled the freshness of her, close up, and was aware suddenly of his own travel and time stained body. She jerked the string abruptly and tightly, to trap Steele's finger in the knot. Of course, he could have pulled back – had he wanted to. But for long seconds he allowed her to hold him a prisoner. Their heights were almost the same and her level gaze was as much his captor as the knot. The mischievous glint was at once transformed into a slow burning wantonness,

'Jessica!'

The man stepped through the curtain as he snapped out the name. Steele jerked his finger free and tore his eyes away from those of the woman. The man was about sixty, short and very thin. He was dressed in an Eastern-style black suit and wore a stiff-collared white shirt and a necktie. His face was long and angular, with sucked in cheeks and deep-set eyes. Many lines of time and anxiety rutted his mottled skin. His black hair, thick and healthy-looking, seemed incongruous as a crown to his emaciated appearance. Only in the height of the forehead and set of the jaw did he and Jessica bear a family resemblance.

'Yes, father?' The woman's voice held a note of annoyance.

Benson's eyes were heavy with suspicion as they surveyed Steele. Then, when the examination was complete, they showed the distaste of a bad first impression. 'I'll tend the store now. You get to the household chores.'

'I'll just finish with this customer, father,' Jessica answered sharply and it was very evident that her resentment was in danger of exploding into anger.

'Do as I say, child!' Benson retorted, bustling towards his daughter aggressively. 'Fire needs building up.'

She seemed about to extend the argument, then shrugged and stepped back from the counter to allow her father to halt between herself and Steele. 'The gentleman had six cartons of forty-fours and two of forty-ones,' she said quickly, then turned and glided towards the curtained archway, swaying her hips and rustling her petticoats.

Benson stared after her, his face flushing as he held his temper on a short rein. When he turned to face Steele his dark eyes continued to hold their fixed glare. 'Be ten dollars, mister,' he snapped.

'Seems to be on the high side,' Steele replied softly.

'We're a long way from any place else,' Benson came back testily. 'I got shipping costs to pay. And the turnover's low. Endsville folks don't do a lot of shooting.'

He rested a skeletal, blue-veined hand on the package, staking his ownership of it until the goods were paid for. Steele took out his newly-earned bankroll and peeled off a ten dollar bill. Benson took the money with bad grace.

'Blood money, but legal tender,' he growled. He pushed the neatly-tied package across the counter and Steele picked it up, along with the rifle.

'Only one of them was dead, and I didn't kill him,' Steele said.

'None of my business,' Benson replied, putting the bill in a cash drawer. 'I just sell the guns and cartridges. What folks do with them ain't my concern.'

'That must help you sleep nights,' Steele told him evenly.

'No man with a daughter like mine sleeps nights, mister,' Benson growled. 'But I got hopes. Jessica's spoken for by young Huntley over at the express office.'

Steele smiled. 'Point taken,' he said softly.

'That's fine,' Benson replied, his tone still hard. 'This ain't a drifter's town, mister. You head east for twenty miles you'll come to Nogales. You'll pay market prices for cartridges. And there's plenty of cheap women there as well.'

'Grateful to you,' Steele told the old man. He patted his bulging pocket and smiled. 'But I can afford better than cheap.'

The old man glared after his customer as Steele stepped out of the cool gloom of the store and on to the sunlit sidewalk. The street was more thickly populated now. Wagons rolled in both directions. Horses waited patiently at hitching rails. Children played and men and women weaved between the running forms. A small group stood in front of the express office, looking expectantly out along the trail curving in from the west.

Once more Steele was conscious of a fearfulness about the people who came close to him as he moved along the bright, hot street, heading for the hotel. He sensed furtive glances in his direction, but these came from a distance. Those citizens of Endsville who veered away from him pointedly avoided meeting his dark-eyed, open gaze. He smiled, but the expression was not an attempt to ease the highly-charged atmosphere that seemed to surround him like some invisible shroud, setting him apart and alone on the busy street. Instead, it was the physical manifestation of laughter directed at himself. Despite his decision to ignore the predictions of Pedro, he had allowed himself to be influenced by them. Because of the apprehensive attitude of the citizens of Endsville he had thought of himself as a harbinger of death giving off signals which were recognisable to others.

But it was nothing so mystical as that, of course. Countless pairs of eyes had watched his bizarre entrance into town. And those who had not actually witnessed the tableau would undoubtedly have heard about it – probably embroidered in the telling. It was therefore quite natural that he should be viewed with fear.

The desk clerk in the sparsely furnished but spotlessly clean lobby of the hotel was as much effected by Steele's presence as everyone else in town – with the exception of Benson and the old man's daughter.

'Room, sir?' He had a pale face and a squint in one eye. His hands shook as he turned the register and thrust a pen towards Steele.

'The best you have,' Steele replied evenly. 'Best at the front, anyway.'

'It's quieter at the rear of the hotel, sir,' the clerk replied as Steele signed the register.

He used his own name, signing with a confident flourish. Endsville was almost a continent away from where he had killed Bish. The Pinkerton detective did not have him listed as wanted and Sheriff White did not have a poster on him.

'Front.' Steele's tone was low and polite.

The clerk's squint was abruptly more pronounced and he whirled quickly to pluck a key from a bank of pigeon holes. He dropped it on the open register. 'Number seven on the second floor. Bathroom's at the end of the hall.' He gulped and hurried on. 'That's if you'd like to take a bath, sir.'

Steele nodded. 'No offence taken,' he assured the clerk as he picked up the key. 'Relax, uh?'

'Yes, sir,' the clerk replied, as tense as ever.

Steele could sense the eyes fastened on him in a nervous stare as he moved up the steep stairway rising from the rear of the lobby. The hotel was quiet and smelled clean. His room was also clean, with a neatly made-up bed, a clothes closet, a dresser with a Bible on top and a chair. It had a partially opened window which looked out over the entrance porch and across the street junction towards the law office and gaolhouse, sandwiched between the saloon and express company depot. He saw the sheriff and the moon-faced youngster standing in the law office doorway then noticed a stirring among the knot of six or seven men and women in front of the depot. He opened the window wider and craned out to look along the street and the trail beyond. A stage was heading for town, moving at a sedate pace that raised little dust and no steam from the backs of the six horse team.

Steele watched it all the way to a halt outside the depot and inevitably the waiting group swelled. For in a town as isolated as Endsville, the arrival of a regular stage was one of the few diversions. From his elevated vantage point, Steele had a good view of the disembarking passengers. Two elderly women, a young couple with a baby and two men. The women and family were warmly greeted by friends and relatives and there was a great deal of interest in the mail sack passed down from the roof rack to the depot manager. Nobody was pleased to see the two men and, in fact, they received similar treatment to that which the citizens had given Steele. But to a lesser degree. Distaste rather than fear prevented the people from looking at the men more than fleetingly.

For their part, the men appeared uncaring of what the townspeople thought of them. Both glanced around at the crowd, seeking a familiar face. They exchanged a few words when they failed to find what they were looking for, then ambled to the rear of the stage to untie their horses. The centre of interest was now within the depot, where the manager had taken the mail sack. Those people not expecting to receive anything dispersed to continued their interrupted business.

'You looking for Turner and the Thorntons?' Sheriff White called.

Steele looked away from the two newcomers and at the doorway of the law office. The fat sheriff was no longer leaning against the jamb at ease. He pulled himself rigidly to his full height and was holding a Spencer rifle across his chest. His finger was curled around the trigger but the muzzle pointed at the clear blue sky. The men halted in the process of mounting, held the position for a few moments, then swung into their saddles.

'Reckon you know the answer to that,' one of them replied. 'Else you wouldn't have asked.'

Both men were about thirty, tall and powerfully built. They were dressed in dark pants, shirts and wide-brimmed hats. Their skin was also dark, from long exposure to the elements and seemed to have a texture that matched the crinkled leather of their ancient riding boots. Both had piercing blue eyes and long, unkempt hair. Both wore a Colt in a tied down holster – Dave Street wore his on the right and Arnie Duff carried his on the left. Steele knew who the men were from the descriptions in the red notebook. The clinching details were the noticeable limp of Duff's right leg and the purple birthmark at the side of Street's nose.

'Turner's dead,' the lawman announced and the two wanted men did not even blink in reaction. 'I got the Thorntons in – '

'Hey, Arnie, Dave, we're in here.' The shout came from the tiny barred window of the cell facing the street. It was Fred Thornton's voice, bright and cheerful.

Duff and Street both looked towards the window and surprise showed fleetingly on their faces. Then both grinned and raised their hands in greeting. Neither man moved closer so that voices continued to be raised, carrying clearly to where Steele stood.

'You and Al got took by him?' Duff called, jerking a thumb towards White. He made it blatantly obvious that his derision was aimed at the overweight lawman.

'Nah, you know White,' Fred answered. 'He don't go looking for trouble. Bounty hunter kinda took us unawares.'

'And killed Jake?' Street wanted to know.

'Nah. That was a Pinkerton cop. But we got him.'

'Bounty hunter still around?' Duff asked, and his tone was suddenly harsh, demanding. He fixed his piercing stare upon the sheriff.

'Wouldn't know,' White answered shortly.

'Over to the hotel,' Fred Thornton called. 'I seen him go there,

67

just a while back.' He thrust an arm through the bars. 'Hey, I can see him from here.'

A finger pointed from the end of the arm, drawing a bead upon Steele. The eyes of Duff and Street swung to look in the same direction. White and Zeke looked at the window, too. And many other pairs of eyes, for the loud voiced exchange had been overheard by many people on the street. But Steele concentrated upon returning the curious gazes of the two wanted men.

'He don't look much,' Street announced after a few moments of tense silence.

'He had some luck,' Thornton allowed. Then his harsh laughter quivered in the hot air. 'Glad he did. This place is cheaper than the hotel. Food's good, too.'

'You're okay in there for a while?' Duff asked.

'Sure thing, Arnie. Me and Al are doin' fine.'

'Not just for a while,' White barked, lowering the rifle a little but still pointing it at the sky. Zeke backed into the shadowed interior of the office. 'They're staying locked up in the cells until the circuit judge gets here.'

'Sure,' Duff said, patronisingly.

'I mean it!' Now the fat man's voice was a snarl.

'We'll talk about it after we've dealt with the bounty hunter,' Street said. He had not taken his eyes off Steele since first spotting him. He spat out of the corner of his mouth, still staring fixedly at the man in the hotel window.

'You got business with him, get it done outside the town limits,' White snarled. 'Won't none of your kind thank you if you make trouble in Endsville.'

'Won't none of our kind thank you for locking up Fred and Al,' Duff countered, and now he swung his gaze back to Steele, his blue eyes glinting in anticipation. 'But we know the score, sheriff. And we ain't about to stink up the town with the blood of a bounty hunter.' He raised his voice. 'You hear me, bounty hunter?'

Steele nodded, not altering his nonchalant expression. 'Clearly as a bell,' he called down.

Street spat again. 'You either ride outta town or we drag you out. Either way, you're dead at the end.'

Duff laughed. 'And we'll all be hearing that bell clear. Tolling for you, bounty hunter.'

'You got until ten o'clock tonight,' Street called.

Steele pursed his lips.

'Okay?' Duff demanded.

'Sure,' Steele replied. 'What I earned for bringing in your buddies ought to last out until then. With enough over to pay my way to Laramie.'

Street and Duff wrenched their gazes away from the window to stare at each other. Duff was the first one to laugh and the sound was a harsh taunt of derision. Then Street's mouth sprang open to gush out his own brand of mockery.

'Christ!' he exploded. 'He figures to pick up the bounty on us!'

Duff curtailed his laughter abruptly and his voice became a snarl. 'You got a goddamn nerve!' he yelled.

'Of Steele,' the grey-haired man at the window called in reply, and showed his teeth in a gentle grin.

Then, with a fast, fluid motion that made his actions a blur, he snapped up the rifle. There was a gasp from many throats which in the next split-second was swamped by the double crack of two shots, so close together they almost formed a single sound. Duff and Street both clawed at their revolvers as they kicked free of their stirrups. But when they hit the street, each with a yell of angry shock, they saw that Steele had lowered the rifle and was looking down at them with studied coolness.

Both men ripped their hats off their heads and glared at the neat holes, one drilled through each brim. Street found his voice first, swinging his head to look up at the window.

'What the hell?' he roared.

'You warned me,' Steele replied evenly. 'Only fair you should know what you're up against.'

Duff recovered enough self-assurance to inject mockery into his tone. 'An honourable bounty hunter yet!' he yelled.

'Always was a straight shooter,' Steele responded before slamming down the window.

Chapter Seven

STEELE took a bath with the derringer under-and-over resting atop his clothes piled at the side of the tub. Then he shaved and dressed as far as his underwear, pants and shirt. He placed the chair under the doorknob inside his room and then pushed the hard, narrow bed against the wall with the window in it. But back from the window, in a corner. When he was stretched out on the bed he could not see out of the window and therefore there was no clear shot at him from outside. He slept with the derringer in his left hand and his right hand curled around the rifle. For the first time in over a month the sleep was completely natural, thrust upon him by genuine fatigue instead of the brain dulling effect of alcohol.

Hunger woke him and when he snapped open his eyes the room was only slightly less dark than the blanket of blackness that had existed behind his closed lids. Night had crept in from the surrounding mountains to drape the basin in which Endsville nestled. It was a night without moon or stars for heavy cloud cover marked the heavens. Steele raised himself from the bed and went to the window. He looked down at the junction and then along the streets which formed it. The town was doing little to combat the darkness. The saloon, law office, hotel and restaurant spilled yellow wedges from windows. And farther out towards the outskirts of town, a few houses showed lights. Up at the ranch a few squares of yellow were painted on the black background of the spread. But that was all. Endsville was an early-to-bed town.

A few eddies of dust rose from the surface of the street. The wind looked gentle, but cold. He cracked open the window to test the weather and discovered it was as chill as it looked as a draught knifed into the room. He put on his boots, scarf, coat and hat. Then he removed the chair from the door and left the room, carrying the rifle ready. In the lobby, the desk clerk looked up from reading a newspaper as he heard Steele's tread on the stairway. Even in the lamplight he had the squint. A nervous licking of his lips added further involuntary animation to his pasty face as Steele approached him.

'You have an hotel safe big enough to store this?' Steele asked, placing the Colt Hartford carefully on the desk.

The clerk shook his head. 'No, sir. But I'll be here on duty all night. I'll take care of it for you.'

'Grateful,' Steele told him, swinging around to head for the door.

It was closed against the weather. The biting wind snapped around Steele as he stepped outside. He looked along North Street, then up and down East and West. He was alone out in the open. There were not even any horses hitched to the rails positioned at intervals along the sidewalk edges. The wind sighed between the buildings and business signs creaked as they swung to and fro. There were no other sounds in the entire basin until he began to move along the sidewalk. Then his footfalls rang hollowly on the planking. His tread was less loud on the rippling dust of the street. On the opposite side his progress was once more blatantly announced with each tread he took. The door of the law office was cracked open as he drew level. He halted but neither turned nor drew his hands from his pockets.

'Something you ought to know, Steele,' Sheriff White hissed.

'Listening,' Steele replied softly, glancing along the street to where a clock outside the hardware store showed the time at eight-thirty.

'It's against the law to let off firearms inside city limits,' White told him.

'Going to arrest me?'

'Warning you not to do it again.'

'Because you've only got two cells and both of them are occupied?' Steele suggested, turning his head to show the lawman a grin.

'Won't be that way for long!' Fred Thornton called mockingly.

Steele saw the tension in White's fleshy face. Beyond him, at the back of the law office, the moon-faced Zeke seemed to be trembling. He had a deputy's badge pinned to his shirt. And he wore a gunbelt and held a Spencer rifle.

'You brought trouble to this town,' White accused, hissing the words between clenched teeth. Then he slammed the door.

Steele moved on down the street, then halted abruptly again as a moist sound was stamped upon all the others. A splash of spittle stained the sidewalk at his feet and he looked up and to his right. The elder Thornton's face was a mask of hatred in the barred window of his cell.

'You ain't popular, mister,' he rasped, then emitted a gust of raucous laughter. 'Not popular at all. When they bury you tomorrow won't be nobody there to mourn.'

'That's my funeral,' Steele said and moved on by the window.

As he passed the batswing doors of the saloon he glanced in without stopping. It was not a large place, but it looked cavernous because it was so poorly patronised. A man was standing at the bar, drinking whiskey and wearing a morose expression. Steele recognised him as the express depot manager and wondered idly if he was John Huntley – who had spoken for Jessica Benson. Behind the scarred counter a short, fat, elderly bartender stared into space, thinking sad thoughts. Street and Duff sat on opposite sides of a table with a bottle of whiskey between them. Each held a glass and a cheroot. A pall of blue smoke was suspended above them, like a cloud of gloom. But they both showed evil grins as they saw Steele pass by.

'What's the time, Arnie?' Street asked very loudly.

Steele had time to see Duff root in his pocket for a watch

before he was beyond the doorway. But the man's reply reached out into the street.

'Getting late, Dave. Running out for a certain bounty hunter.'

In contrast to the saloon, the restaurant was brightly lit and looked inviting. It had ten tables, each spread with a chequered cloth and individually illuminated with an oil lamp at the centre. An elderly waitress stood at the rear and a lone woman customer sat at a window table, drinking coffee. She looked up as Steele entered and he recognised the pretty features of Jessica Benson. There was a moment of depression across her face, and then her eyes lit with a smile that quickly spread to her lips and produced dimples in her cheeks.

'Please join me, Mr Steele,' she said warmly.

He shook his head. 'You join me, miss,' he countered, closing the door and heading towards the rear left hand corner of the restaurant.

He stood behind a chair to wait for the woman to cross the restaurant and sit down opposite him. Then he sat, positioned so that he could see both the front door and windows and the entrance from the kitchen. Jessica had brought her coffee with her and she sipped at it while Steele gave his order to the waitress.

'You have no need to worry, Mr Steele,' Jessica said with a toss of her head that set her pigtails swinging.

'About what?' he asked, unbuttoning his coat and hanging his hat on a wall peg.

'Being attacked in here.' She shrugged. 'Or anywhere in town for that matter. Street and Duff wouldn't dare.'

The waitress shuffled out of the kitchen and delivered a bowl of chicken soup at the table. Steele tasted it and it was good. He decided that after so long without food anything edible would taste good. 'Not because of Sheriff White,' he said.

She showed him a cynical smile. 'Nobody in Endsville does anything because of him.'

Steele's dark eyes became thoughtful as he spooned soup into his mouth. 'This morning, Street said something about knowing the score.'

Jessica nodded. 'He meant about keeping Endsville clear of

trouble. This is a safe town, Mr Steele. For the people who live here and . . . anyone who comes to stay or passes through.'

Her green eyes examined the blandly handsome face beneath the close-cropped, prematurely grey hair. They asked tacitly whether he understood what she was saying.

'White never had anybody locked in his gaol before,' Steele supplied as he finished the first course.

The waitress disappeared into the kitchen.

'Some people who pass through – even stay for a while – are the worst kind of human animal, Mr Steele. Border towns attract that sort. Mostly that means that border towns are trouble. But not Endsville. It's something that's been established over a long time. A . . . '

'Tradition,' Steele offered as the waitress delivered a plate of beef stew and took away the empty soup bowl.

Jessica nodded. 'Yes. One that's always been honoured. Unwritten law. They come here and don't bother the townspeople. And the law doesn't bother them. If a marshal comes to town, they just go through the pass into Mexico.'

'And bounty hunters?' Steele asked. The soup had taken the edge off his hunger, but still the beef stew was good.

'The regular ones obey the unwritten law,' Jessica replied. 'Which means you've got to be new to this part of the country.'

'New to the job,' Steele replied, reflecting upon Sheriff White's attitude. 'And I seem to have presented the local law with a new situation.'

Jessica's smile now was of pure pleasure. 'You've scared the hell out of Sheriff White,' she confirmed. 'He's never had the guts to try to establish regular law over the unwritten one. Now you've forced it upon him and he's got to make a choice between doing his job as he ought to and backing down from Street and Duff.'

'Death or dishonour,' Steele put in softly.

'That's very right,' she confirmed. 'The sheriff's suddenly realised he's got principles. He's never had to face up to that kind of problem before.'

'You aren't just talking to fill in time,' Steele said after a ngthy pause.

She stared down into her empty cup and Steele finished his stew. He asked her if she wanted more coffee and when she nodded he passed on the request to the waitress and ordered a cup for himself.

'You're getting around to something,' he prodded when the steaming, aromatic cups were set down.

She sipped at her drink and burned her tongue. The pain spurred her into an answer. 'You're going to have to kill Duff and Street or they'll kill you, Mr Steele.'

He sighed. 'Could be, Miss Benson.'

'I don't think you're easy to kill.'

'It's been tried,' he allowed.

'So you'll leave Endsville.'

He nodded. 'For Laramie. When the time's right.'

Jessica's expression became grim. 'The time is right now, Mr Steele. White is going to make a stand. I'm sure of it. He's going to try to bring the Thorntons to trial. Whether he succeeds or not doesn't matter as far as you're concerned. Every outlaw in the south west is going to come looking for the man who ruined Endsville for him.'

'Which is me?'

'That's very right. The word could be out already. I think you should leave now. As soon as you finish your coffee.'

'And . . . ' He allowed the word to hang in the quietness of the restaurant.

'Take me with you, Mr Steele,' she said quickly, urgently. She leaned towards him, giving him a close-up of the pleading look in her green eyes.

'You're spoken for, Miss Benson,' Steele told him lightly.

She shook her head violently, the pigtails flying. 'My father thinks so. And John. But I'm not a little girl any more. I'm old enough to make up my own mind. And I've made it up. To see what's on the other side of the mountains before I decide whether I want to marry – John Huntley or anybody.'

Steele tried the coffee and could not recall tasting a cup that was better. 'Stage was through here this morning,' he said.

She grimaced. 'I've tried to escape this town three times on my own. South is Mexico and that's too dangerous for an

American woman. In every other direction there are just scattered farms and way stations for almost twenty miles. And everyone on them knows my father well enough . . . to know he'd never give me permission to leave.'

'I know him that well now,' Steele told her.

His easy attitude angered her. 'Why the hell should you give a damn?' she yelled. 'You don't have to come back here – ever!'

She was suddenly embarrassed by her outburst and looked around anxiously. But the waitress had gone into the kitchen. She looked back at Steele and the expression in her eyes became sensuous. She rested a hand gently on his and her voice was low and husky. 'I'd be very grateful to you, Mr Steele,' she said, and squeezed his hand. She lowered her voice still further. 'You can even have a down payment on my gratitude, if you want,' she offered.

The waitress had left the check when she brought the coffee. It totalled five dollars, which was as exorbitant as the prices Jessica's father charged. Steele guessed the waitress would rationalise the extortion with the same argument put forward by Benson. He slid a five spot under his cup and added no tip. When he stood up, the woman eyed him anxiously.

'Well?' she asked.

'A gentleman never turns down a lady,' Steele replied, and ushered her to her feet.

He put on his hat and buttoned his coat, then took her hooded cape from a peg near the door and helped her on with it. Outside, the night was colder, the wind stronger. Low cloud scudded across the sky at breakneck speed. Dust stung their faces. Signs creaked and then banged at the limit of their swings. Jessica said something to him, but the whine of the wind masked her words and he leaned closer.

'I don't want to go in the front entrance, Mr Steele,' she shouted in his ear. 'The desk clerk owes my father a favour. There's a back door.'

Steele nodded, then allowed her to take his arm and lead him along West Street, away from the hotel. They went beneath the clock outside the hardware store and he saw it pointed the time nine fifteen. Where the sidewalk ended beyond the business centre of town, Jessica angled out into the street and crossed to the other side. She continued to take the initiative, steering him back towards the junction on the corner of which the hotel was sited. She quickened the pace and their footfalls on the sidewalk were muffled by the whine of the wind between the buildings. She stayed very close to him, so that their hips constantly bumped.

When they were opposite the restaurant he saw that the waitress was back in position, standing silent guard over the empty tables. Crossing North Street he could see across the junction and into the saloon. The depot manager was still drinking without joy while the bartender contemplated infinity. The table where Street and Duff had sat was now vacant.

Jessica led him across the street on a diagonal course, which brought them to a gap in the sidewalk that offered access to a wide alley at the side of the hotel. Apart from sparse light which filtered from the lobby doorway on the corner, North Street was in complete darkness. It was pitch black in the alley and the wind made an eerie whistling sound as it rushed through the gap. Jessica tightened her grip on his arm and pressed harder against him as they stepped into the alley. The wind hit them full in the face and they bent into it.

That sense of another's presence which is possessed by the vast majority of human beings, warned Steele an instant too late. He was mid-way through a stride and had to complete it to get his balance. Because of the forward canting of his body, his chest came into contact with the rope which was stretched from one side of the alley to the other. Jessica's thrusting breasts touched the rope at the same instant as Steele jerked free of her grip. She screamed, thrust to one side as Steele sprang the other way.

But Street and Duff held on to the split-second advantage of surprise. Street powered away from the hotel side of the alley, keeping the rope taut as he thrust his arms into the air. Duff went forward in a crouched run from the side of a bakery, hauling on his end of the rope. As the two men passed they completed a circle of rope around Steele and the woman. And they continued to run, jerking the rope to tighten the circle.

77

Steele and Jessica were slammed back against each other again and the woman emitted another scream. Of pain this time, as the viciously tightened rope bit into the firm swells of her breasts. The sound became injected with terror as she found herself lifted from her feet, kicking helplessly in midair, held against Steele's arched back.

Steele heard the scream close to his ear and grunted with pain as the rope constricted around his chest. But he continued to go down, bending at the knees to gape the slit in his right pants leg. His fingers curled around the handle of the knife and the blade came free of the boot sheath just as Duff ran around the front of him. He straightened up, slamming Jessica to the ground, and slashed the knife edge across the rope. The honed blade sliced through the rope like a razor on cotton.

Immediately, the constriction was relieved. Jessica slumped to the ground and began to sob. Duff had been using the rope to hold himself on to his headlong, circular course. The moment the knife cut him loose, centrifugal force powered him into an uncontrolled dive. He crashed into the frame side of the bakery and roared in agony.

Steele could not see him in the shadows, but accepted the sound of pain as an indication that the man presented no immediate threat. So he whirled towards Street, unaware of the identity of either man. Street had fared better than his partner when the rope parted. He, too, had been pitched involuntarily forward, but not against the side of a building. Instead, he had been forced into a staggering run along the alley, fighting to stay on his feet. He succeeded, and swung around in a half crouch as Steele spun to face him. He could see nothing but a wall of darkness. Steele could see him as a black silhouette against the dim, filtered light that curtained the mouth of the alley.

Street wasted a precious moment considering the implications of breaking the unwritten law of Endsville against the immediate need for self-preservation. The latter consideration won and he clawed for his Colt. He dragged the gun clear of the holster and levelled it.

'Christ, Dave, don't!' Duff screamed. Fear was a tremor in voice, but there was no way of knowing whether the plea was made on behalf of saving himself from a wild shot or a warning of the repercussions.

It served to freeze Street's finger on the trigger as the knife spun towards him. Steele hurled it underarm, as he came up from his whirling crouch. It was delivered with all the compact power contained in his arm from shoulder to wrist. The point penetrated Street's coat sleeve just above the crooked elbow and sank into the flesh. He screamed, releasing his grip on the gun and staring down at the quivering knife. The point hit his bone and the blade was deflected, bursting clear at the side of his arm. The entry wound was widened to gush a spout of blood as a second spray erupted from the side of his arm, drenching his coat sleeve.

Steele had leapt across Jessica's crumpled, sobbing form, the moment he released the knife. But Duff was too quick for him. With fear surmounting pain, he launched himself upright and lunged into a panicked run into the depths of the alley. Street heard the pumping footfalls above the whine of the wind and the choking sobs of the woman. And he knew he was being deserted to face Steele alone. For a moment he was rooted to the spot, staring down at the ugliness of the knife skewered through his arm. Then he turned and broke into an ungainly, zigzagging run, clutching at his injured arm above the wound. He burst out into North Street and staggered into a left turn, away from the meagre lighting of the junction.

Steele stared at the empty mouth of the alley for a moment, then peered in the other direction. The wind roared at him from out of the darkness but brought no threat with it. He moved away from the wall of the bakery and crouched down on his haunches beside the woman. He put his mouth close to her ear.

'They've gone, Miss Benson,' he said evenly.

She stopped sobbing and looked up at him from under the cape hood. Her face was merely a pale splash against the dark hood. Her eyes were liquid pools with a lot more tears ready to spill.

'Who were they?' she asked. 'Duff and Street?'

'Maybe,' Steele answered as he helped her gently to her feet. 'Certainly no friends of your father.'

Her lids blinked across the surface of the pools of her eyes and splashed salty droplets across her cheeks. 'What is that supposed to mean?' she demanded, on the verge of anger.

Steele grinned as he held up a length of the severed rope. 'Tried to get you tied up with the wrong man,' he replied.

Chapter Eight

THEY entered the hotel through the back entrance, which gave on to a laundry room with a stairway reaching up to the first floor. Steele took the initiative now, leading Jessica lightly by the arm. She had stopped crying, but occasionally a spasm of trembling gripped her as she continued to react to the shock of the attack.

The first floor hallway was dimly lit by a lamp with the wick turned low. The key to room seven was downstairs with the desk clerk, but the door swung open with only a slight pressure of Steele's shoulder against the panel. Inside, a faint glow spilled in through the window, picked up from the lights in the restaurant, saloon and sheriff's office across the junction. There were no curtains to filter it nor drapes to mask it.

Jessica stood in the centre of the small room and chewed her lower lip while Steele wedged the chair back under the door handle. Her features were more clearly defined in the gentle lighting and she looked very young again. Vulnerable. And her eyes were no longer liquid pools. Rather they resembled empty sockets. With fear lurking in their depths. Steele eyed her reflectively for long moments, then started across the room. She flinched and stepped back. He kept on going, to the window, and looked out. Eddying dust and swinging signs were all that moved below. In the pale glow of light anyway. There were enough dark shadows to conceal an army. Steele turned and rested his rump on the sill, pushing his hat on to the top of his head and folding his arms.

'You've changed your mind, Miss Benson?' he asked softly.

'Not about leaving Endsville,' she replied, still pressing herself back against the wall.

'But about paying the fare in advance?'

She didn't answer for a moment, and looked to her left and right with distaste. 'It's a nasty little room,' she said.

'I could have had the best, but that's at the rear of the hotel,' Steele told her.

'And it's cold,' she complained, hugging herself in confirmation.

'Like you?' His voice was suddenly harsh and she flinched again.

He challenged her with his stare and she looked away. But then she gained courage and locked her stare on his. She unfolded her arms and loosened the tie at her throat. 'If you won't take me without,' she snapped, and shrugged out of the cape.

Despite his change of tone, Steele's expression had remained nonchalant ever since entering the room. His features held their blandness as he watched the woman start to unfasten the buttons which held her dress together from neckline to waist. She continued to glare at him, with her lips pressed firmly together. Her free hand held the bodice of the dress together until all the buttons to the waist had been unfastened. Then she gripped the fabric at each side and jerked them apart dramatically. She wore nothing underneath and her large, unfettered breasts thrust erotically into full view. She breathed in deeply to prevent sag and the cold of the room rather than desire caused the nipples to extend firmly from the large patches of dark aureoles. He broke from the glare to look at her upper body and then his gaze dropped lower as the woman inserted her hands into the waistband of the dress. She gyrated her hips and the dress and her underwear slid over them and encircled her feet. Her well-formed legs tapered up from the froth of material, thickening into strong thighs. Where they met her gently curved stomach the triangle of hair was just slightly darker than the milky whiteness of her flesh.

'You can see I'm a woman who means what she says, Mr Steele,' she said huskily when Steele's eyes returned to her face.

Some of the nonchalance had gone from his expression now. In the dim light, his eyes glinted, mirroring the excitement stirring within his body. 'I can see you're a woman,' he replied.

A smile of gentle satisfaction turned up the corners of Jessica's mouth. She stepped demurely out of the discarded dress, sat on the edge of the narrow bed and lifted her legs on to it. She rested her head back on the pillow and lay with her legs pressed together and arms at her sides.

'You said a gentleman never turned one down,' she reminded him.

Steele turned sideways on to the window to look along the length of her naked body. He shook his head. 'I said lady, Miss Benson. And you're no lady.'

Her head snapped up angrily, but then she saw the desire in his eyes had strengthened. The smile returned and she lifted an arm and crooked a finger at him. 'And you're no gentleman, Mr Steele,' she countered, slowly lowering her head back on the pillow as she parted her thighs in invitation.

The crash of the opening door was like a thunderclap against the instant of silence that had clamped over the room after the woman's final word. There was the thud of a shoulder against the panel, the crunch of the chair splintering and the thump of the door against the wall. All merged into one sound that was drowned into insignificance by the shrillness of Jessica's scream.

Steele leapt backwards, taking his silhouette out of the square of light in the window. His hand delved into his coat pocket and curled around the butt of the tiny under-and-over. He dropped into a crouch and swung around to face the doorway, pressing the twin muzzles of the derringer against the pocket lining. Jessica screamed again, but the timbre of the sound spoke of a different kind of fear. She rolled on to her side, drew up her legs and curled her body, hugging herself into a ball.

Her father halted abruptly, silhouetted starkly against the meagre light in the hallway. Enough glow from the window reached across the room to reveal the volatile mixture of anger and despair painted on the rutted flesh of his lean face. His dark eyes, pulled wide, swung from Jessica to Steele and then back to his daughter again. His thin lips opened and closed soundlessly several times before he was able to force out the words.

'You brazen hussy!' he rasped.

His tone of voice and his expression made the accusation sound like an obscenity. Steele thought the old man had a foul-mouthed insult in mind but could not bring himself to voice it. His daughter buried her face in her hands and began to sob and Benson swung to face Steele, who had straightened up and allowed the tenseness to drain from his body.

'Nothing happened, Mr Benson,' he said softly.

The storekeeper raised a shaking hand and pointed to the trembling nakedness of his daughter. 'You call this nothing?' he demanded.

Steele sighed, retaining his grip on the derringer. Benson was not wearing a gun in sight. But neither was Steele. 'Could have been worse,' he replied evenly.

'If Mrs Clarke over the restaurant hadn't watched you bring Jessica into the hotel by the back way. And hadn't warned me. And I hadn't come when I did.' The words were spat out in the manner of a preacher filled with righteous anger.

'That's a lot of negatives, Mr Benson,' Steele said. 'And I'm not a fortune teller.' He looked coldly towards the sobbing woman. 'I have to admit, though. I am a man.'

Benson made a sound of disgust deep in his throat, and snapped his head around to stare at Jessica. 'Get dressed!' he ordered.

Then he swung around, turning his back on the woman. Steele chose to look out of the window and, as if in like deference to Jessica's modesty, the lights of the junction went out. First those in the restaurant, then in the law office and finally the saloon was darkened. The last, only after the tall, gangling, slightly unsteady figure of John Huntley had pushed through the bats-wings and started along West Street.

Jessica's sobs were less frequent now as she made small noises pulling on her clothes.

'I want you to know,' Benson said suddenly, his voice calmer, colder.

Steele transferred his indifferent gaze from the darkened streets to the storekeeper.

'I revile you for your lack of self-restraint,' the old man continued. 'But I got no doubt my daughter led you on.'

'Makes me feel a whole lot better to know that,' Steele said wryly.

Benson ignored the tone. 'Got a wanton streak in her. Her mother never had it, God rest her. And I've always kept the Commandments. Guess she's what they call a throwback.'

'Nobody's perfect,' Steele said, and returned his attention to the cold night outside the window. His eyes flicked over the woman, who was fastening the bodice of her dress. But she was looking at Steele with an expression close to relief in her green eyes. She was a split-second too late in masking it and forcing out a sob.

Steele thought he saw someone moving in the deep shadows in front of the law office: a blur of something pale in the dark. But then Jessica's voice captured his attention.

'I'm ready now.'

Both men looked at her and saw that she was fully dressed, encased in the hooded cape.

'Then we'll go home,' her father announced, stepping to the side to allow her passage to the doorway. He looked at her with revulsion as she went by him. Then his eyes swung towards Steele, filled with cold hatred. 'The sooner you leave this town, the better it will be for everyone in it,' he said, and hurried out of the room to catch up with his daughter.

Steele pursed his lips as he saw his reflection in the window. 'She's right,' he told his image. 'You're no gentleman. Didn't even take your hat off.'

He heard footfalls below on the sidewalk and leaned closer to the pane, blotting out his reflection to watch the couple as they moved away from the hotel. They walked at a distance from each other, both rigidly erect and staring directly ahead. And too concerned with their own thoughts to be aware of the flare of light that splashed the darkness in front of the law office. Steele saw it on the periphery of his vision and swung his eyes for a wide angle view as the flame of the fuse touched the pack of explosive powder.

The flash was bright yellow streaked with orange and for a split-second lit up the junction as clearly as the mid-day sun. The roar was powerful enough to rattle the window where Steele stood and the hotel trembled. He gripped the sill to steady himself but despite this his vision was blurred for a moment. When it cleared, the brightness of the initial blast had faded to be replaced by the flickering light of flames. In this he saw the ugly, jagged black hole which had been ripped in the front wall of the law office. The sidewalk below and the awning above fuelled the fire. A man and a woman were screaming. The man was inside the blasted building and suddenly he burst out through the hole. It was Zeke, the moon-faced kid who had worn a deputy's badge. Now he wore nothing. The blast had ripped the clothing from his frail body. Streaking flame had seared the naked flesh, blackening it so that the teeth in his wide, screaming mouth stood out as twin curves of brilliant white. His right arm hung too low and was much too thin where it became the shoulder. The boy ran no more than half a dozen strides before he died, pitching headlong to the street. He rolled over twice and lay still. Both parts of him. The impact of the dead fall had ripped the final tendons holding his right arm to his body and the limb was left three feet from where his body came to rest.

The woman continued to scream and Steele's unblinking eyes sought out Jessica Benson. She had been flung on to her back and lay spread-eagled. She did not move. Just stared up into the wind-whipped black smoke and held her mouth open to its fullest extent, sending a high-pitched wail into the night. Her father lay ten feet away from her, on his side, knees tucked into his chest. A widening pool of darkness spread around him, soaking into the rock hardness of the street surface. His head emptied more blood on to the thirsty ground, resting twenty feet away from its owner, against a charred section of timber that had severed the neck.

The sound of the explosion had temporarily deafened Steele and he saw the four horses before he heard their hoofbeats. Two were riderless but ready saddled, being led at a gallop by Street and Duff. They rode into the junction from West Street and skidded to a halt in front of the blazing law office. Street's right arm was in a sling. Duff was holding a Colt. Both men were cursing their mounts and the spare horses as the animals reared and snorted at the smoke and fire.

The Thorntons burst out through the jagged hole, coughing violently. They were holding bed mattresses around their bodies, smouldering in places. Then they dropped their protection, snatching the reins of the spare horses from Street and Duff and hauling themselves into the saddles. Duff fired the Colt into the air and all four riders thudded in their heels. The horses reacted with the speed of self-interest, lunging into an immediate gallop away from the fire. The thunder of a dozen hooves drowned out the screaming of Jessica Benson until the distance of East Street swallowed the riders.

And then the confused shouts and running footsteps of Endsville's citizenry filled the night. From East, West and North Streets they poured out of the darkness and into the fringes of the flickering firelight illuminating the scene of mutilated death. But nobody ventured too close. White faced men and women, their night attire cloaked by hurriedly donned coats, formed into a broad horseshoe shape around three sides of the junction. What they saw answered their shouted questions and they became silent. Jessica Benson stopped screaming, started to rise and saw the beheaded form of her father. She fell back into a faint, her head thudding against the hard ground. The wind whined between the buildings and the fanned flames roared.

Steele straightened up from the window and because of the dancing firelight beyond the glass he was unable to see his reflection any more. But he knew the kind of nonchalant expression he showed as he pursed his lips. Below on the junction, people less accustomed to seeing violent death at close quarters, recovered from their shock. They moved hesitantly forward, to help Jessica, to cover the bodies and to put out the fire. Steele, still coolly detached from what had happened, went out of the cold room and along the hallway. From the foot of the stairs he could see the pasty faced desk clerk in the hotel doorway, squinting out into the street.

'Like my rifle,' Steele called.

The man turned, blinked and hurried to go behind his desk.

There was a doorway at the back and he went through it. When he reappeared, carrying the Colt Hartford, Steele was at the desk. The clerk thrust the gun towards its owner, as if anxious to be rid of it.

'You see what happened to Mr Benson?' the nervous man asked.

'I saw,' Steele answered, taking the gun and resting it across his shoulder.

'He always said his daughter would be the death of him,' the clerk said as Steele crossed to the doorway.

'Not the first man to lose his head over a woman,' Steele replied evenly as he went out.

Chapter Nine

TROTTER, the town's mortician, drove his hearse into the junction as Steele emerged from the hotel. The man's long face seemed to be concealing an avaricious smile behind its mournful expression as he surveyed the blanket covered forms on the street. His funereal pose almost slipped completely when two men carried the draped body of Sheriff White out of the law office.

The fire was out now and those who had been engaged in tossing water on the flames seemed uncomfortable in idleness. Those who had merely watched looked guilty. Jessica Benson was no longer sprawled on the ground and Steele stepped out on to the street in time to see John Huntley carry the woman into the express company depot. There was plenty of light now, splashing out across the junction from almost every window in the town centre. In it, many pairs of eyes followed Steele's unhurried progress towards the livery stable. But he no longer sensed fear in the watchers. Nor even acrimony. Except from Mrs Clarke who stood in the lighted doorway of her restaurant. But when he swung his head to look at her, the grey haired old woman turned away guiltily. He guessed she was trying to blame him for the tragedy of Benson's death. But that her conscience was accusing her even more strongly for her interference.

He saw the owner of the livery stable was one of a group of middle-aged to elderly men in low-voiced conversation on the sidewalk outside the saloon. Several of these men were watching Steele pensively. The door of the livery was locked and Steele leaned against it in a relaxed pose, waiting for the message to reach the owner. He watched as Trotter and three other men loaded the whole body of White and the broken corpses of Benson and Zeke aboard the hearse. Wind-borne dust coated the blood stains in the street and quickly obliterated them. The hearse made a tight turn and trundled back along North Street with appropriate slowness. The citizenry of the town began to retreat from the scene of the carnage, with the exception of the group of men outside the saloon.

When the junction was empty, they stepped down from the sidewalk and started along the street towards Steele. There were ten of them. In addition to the owner of the livery stable, Steele recognised the bartender from the saloon and two men who had stepped from his path earlier in the day. There was nothing aggressive in the attitude of any of the men, but their number and the measured cadence of their pace which held them in a group caused Steele to tighten his grip on the rifle canted across his shoulder. They halted six feet in front of him and eyed him with a mixture of expressions ranging from the rueful to the kind of melancholy that is close to tears. All around the junction, the lights started to go out again, until only the windows of the saloon and the express depot spilled pale yellow into the streets.

'No trouble, Mr Steele,' the bartender announced, his fat face among the saddest of the group. 'Endsville's been without it for a long time. And we've had enough tonight to make up for all we missed in the past.'

'And for a lot of the future,' a bearded man put in.

'Right,' the bartender agreed.

'The kind of town Sheriff White ran couldn't go on for ever,' Steele replied.

'He knew it and we knew it,' the bartender said with a nod. 'And it worked all right.'

'Until I brought in some trouble on the end of a rope,' Steele suggested.

Some of the men shuffled their feet. They raised dust which the wind snatched away and hurled along West Street. 'You ain't gonna deny it, we sure ain't,' the bartender said. 'But we ain't holding it against you, mister. You did what you figured was right. And it damn well was right, if you hadn't done it for the money. But that's your business. But what you did, it made Sheriff White start acting like a lawman. And it made us on the citizen's committee – and a few other folks – feel a bit better than we have in the past.'

The man with the beard coughed. 'We've been living in a fool's paradise,' he put in. 'Letting outlaws and murderers use this town like ordinary people. Ignoring them because they left us alone. But that ain't no way for decent folks to live.'

'Right,' the bartender confirmed. 'They been leaving us alone because it suited them. But this is our town and what happens in it ought to be because it suits us.'

There was a nodding of heads and a few grunts of assent.

'We just been sweeping our trouble under the carpet and pretending it wasn't there,' the livery stable owner said. 'The sheriff was always telling us that. He said all that trouble would be let loose one day and blow in our faces.'

'He was standing where it did the most harm,' Steele replied.

'And Bob Benson was in no position to duck,' a voice growled.

'Nor that kid Zeke,' another put in.

'We lost three good men,' the bartender said sadly. 'But we ain't blaming you, mister. Sheriff White and Zeke were paid by the town to do a job and died doing it. Bob Benson just got unlucky by being in the wrong place at the wrong time. But we don't want their lives to be wasted.'

'So?' Steele asked.

None of the others felt moved to take the bartender's job as spokesman any more. The sad faced man waited for a few moments, to ensure this. Then he cleared his throat.

'You're leaving town?'

Steele nodded.

'Where you headed?'

'Depends.'

'On where those four go?' He jerked a thumb across the junction and along East Street.

'My business.'

'Which is bounty hunting. Street and Duff are wanted in Laramie for three thousand dollars each.'

The faces of the men formed a wall of determination, challenging Steele to deny his financial interest in the two outlaws.

'I've got them listed,' he said.

'We are prepared to put up five thousand for the pair,' the bartender said. 'You've already been paid for the Thorntons – and Jake Turner.'

Steele pursed his lips. 'Thousand shy of the Laramie price.'

'Laramie's a long ways from here. Cost you at least a thousand in your time taking them up north.'

Steele nodded his agreement. 'Cost you nothing at all to put out the word that Duff and Street broke the unwritten law of Endsville,' he pointed out. 'Every gunslinger that ever took sanctuary in Endsville would go after them.'

'It's never cheap to get self-respect,' the bartender replied. 'Like I said, we don't want those three men to have died for nothing. Be easy to let their own kind take care of Duff and Street. Thorntons, too. But then we'd be back where we started. You want the job, mister?'

'If I say no?' Steele posed.

The bartender shrugged. 'Committee's just nominated me the new sheriff. Come morning we'll put it to the folks and I'll get elected. Then I'll raise a posse and take off after them four.'

'And the posse'll be nothing but a bunch of willing amateurs,' the bearded man pointed out.

Anger flared for a moment in the bartender's eyes. 'We ain't making no appeal to your sympathy, mister,' he said. 'Me and whoever follows me, we'll do our damn best to bring them four back to stand trial. What you're being offered is a business proposition. Take it or leave it.'

Steele was thoughtful for a moment. 'You've considered what could happen if you – or anybody else – brings in those men? Won't only be Duff and Street and the Thorntons who broke the unwritten law.'

'It's been considered,' the bartender replied. 'But that ain't your problem. Either you take the bounty hunting job or you don't. Whichever way, the job'll get done. And we're prepared to face up to the consequences.'

Steele pursed his lips and the men looked anxiously into his expressionless but still pleasant features. 'Laramie *is* a long way,' he said eventually.

'You'll do it?' the bearded man asked.

'I had it in mind anyway,' Steele replied.

Nobody smiled, but there was an almost tangible aura of relief discernible as the men nodded and released pent up breath.

'I'll get your horse, mister,' the livery stable owner said hurriedly, stepping forward.

'Grateful if you'd saddle him,' Steele replied, moving away from the doorway. 'Any of you other gentlemen the banker in this town?'

All eyes turned towards the man with the beard. 'I am,' he announced unnecessarily. 'I'll guarantee the reward until it's raised – if that's what you want.'

Steele smiled. 'Reckon I can trust you all without a marker. You keep a lot of money in the bank?'

All the men were confused by the question. 'That's confidential information,' the banker said at length, his tone determined.

'Maybe not to the men you want me to bring in,' Steele countered. 'The Thorntons and Jake Turner were waiting in Endsville for something. Then Street and Duff came in looking for them. Seems to me they were meeting up for a purpose that wasn't old time's sake. Something important enough to blow the unwritten law to pieces.'

The theory was received in thoughtful silence. Then the banker spoke. 'Sounds reasonable, mister. But they wouldn't touch the bank. Maybe they figured they could do what they did and get away with it by clearing out of the territory. Pull a job and run far enough away so folk'd give up chasing 'em. But they'd know better than to hit the bank, mister. I figure better than three-quarters of the deposits in the bank is outlaw money.

So I reckon it's no use sitting here in Endsville waiting for 'em to come in for bank money.'

All looked hard at Steele, their expressions tacitly backing up the banker's statement.

'It would be a stupid thing to do,' Steele acknowledged. 'So what else brought them all down to this part of the country? Big enough for them to risk getting on the wrong side of every gunsel who used Endsville as a haven?'

'Nothing in town, that's for sure,' a red haired man replied. 'Ain't nobody poor in Endsville. But ain't nobody really rich, either.'

'Stage?' Steele suggested.

'Have to ask Huntley about that,' the banker replied.

'So let's do that,' Steele said as his horse was led out of the livery.

The group parted to allow him through and Steele led the way to the office of the express depot. The men seemed surprised when he knocked on the door.

'Come in,' a voice called and Steele responded.

The room was small and divided into two by a waist high counter. The slats of a wooden barrier extended from the centre of the counter to the ceiling. There was a square aperture in the slats at a midway point. On the door side of the counter was a row of three wooden benches, placed one behind the other, for the convenience of passengers waiting for the stage. Jessica Benson, pale faced and obviously controlling a threatened spasm of shaking, sat hunched up on the front bench. John Huntley was just straightening up from ducking through an open hatchway at one end of the counter. He held a mug of steaming coffee in one hand and a bottle of whiskey in the other.

The citizens' committee stayed bunched in the doorway as Steele crossed the threshold. Jessica eyed him with anguish. Huntley surveyed his visitor with irritation. He was about thirty-five with the kind of face that matched his long, loose-limbed body. A face furrowed by the lines of an easy smile rather than hardship: with eyes that seemed rather vacant and a mouth line that suggested a generous nature. His clothes and hair were clean but untidy. He seemed the kind of man who took things as they came, under normal circumstances. The kind

94

who resented responsibility but accepted it with resignation when it was thrust upon him.

'Yes?' He gave no indication that he was aware of what had happened between Steele and Jessica.

'Like to ask you a question,' Steele said.

Huntley ambled over to the woman and gave her the coffee. As she held the mug in both hands, he poured a slug of whiskey into it. Steele got the impression that Huntley was unable to concentrate on more than one thing at a time.

'Yes?' he said again when his ministering chore was over.

'Express company have any valuable shipments scheduled to pass through this part of the country tonight, Mr Huntley?' Steele asked.

Huntley glanced from the casual expression on Steele's face to the grim looks worn by the men crowded into the doorway. Jessica sipped at the laced coffee. 'I'm not at liberty to give out that kind of information.'

'It's important, John,' the banker said. 'The committee's engaged Mr Steele to bring in those fellers who murdered Jessica's father and the others.'

The woman's eyes grew very round as she studied Steele across the rim of the mug.

'What has that got to do with the express company?' Huntley demanded. He didn't seem to know what to do with his hands and eventually thrust them into his pants pocket.

'Mr Steele reckons the Thorntons and Street and Duff plan to pull a job someplace around here,' the bartender explained. 'Now if they do, and it's an express shipment they intend to hit, be in your company's interest to let Mr Steele have the information he wants.'

Huntley was not so dumb as he looked. His eyes ceased to be vacant and took on a glitter of suspicion. 'In Mr Steele's interest, too,' he said.

Steele nodded. 'Right.'

'But only in helping him to track down the wanted men,' the banker put in hurriedly. 'We're paying him well.'

'Not as well as a half million in gold,' Jessica said into the silence.

Some of the men in the doorway gasped. Huntley ground his teeth together and fought an impulse to whirl towards the woman. Instead, he gave a long sigh and hunched his shoulders as if he were cold. 'That's just great,' he muttered.

Jessica pulled herself very erect on the bench and faced the implied criticism defiantly. 'They killed my father!' she flung at Huntley. 'I don't think anything should stand in the way of bringing them to trial for that, John.'

Huntley looked at the woman for a long time in silence, as if trying to decide what attitude he should adopt. Then his eyes flicked to Steele, the men in the doorway and back to Jessica. In the time this took, he decided the woman had a point.

'It's a shipment of government gold,' he said and Jessica treated him to a gentle smile that did not convince him he was doing the right thing. 'From St Louis to Colorado Crossing on the border west of here. It's to be used to buy out some settlers and build a fort. The express company has the contract to freight it.'

'Why don't the army do its own hauling?' the banker asked, surprised.

Huntley looked sick. 'They thought it would be safer this way. Attract less attention. There are three wagons and a ten man escort in civilian clothes. All officers. Hand picked. It's supposed to be secret.'

'What d'you think, Mr Steele?' the bartender asked.

'When is it scheduled to reach town?' Steele asked.

'It isn't coming through Endsville,' Huntley answered. 'The shipment hasn't touched a town since leaving St Louis. It'll be stopped for the night at Deep Lake now. Tomorrow the wagons will be rolling south west through the High Peaks country. After that, I don't know. It'll be the responsibility of the express agent in Yuma.'

'How far is Deep Lake from here?' Steele wanted to know.

The bartender answered while Huntley was still thinking about the question. 'Fifty miles. North. First half easy riding on the North Trail. Then rough going over high desert terrain.'

'The High Peaks'd be better to set up an ambush,' another member of the citizens' committee said with the tone of one who knew what he was talking about. 'Easy riding for forty

96

miles on North Trail. Then take your pick of any of a hundred canyons and passes,' He shrugged. 'Course, help if you knew the route the gold's taking.'

Everyone looked at Huntley and the express agent shook his head. 'I just know that tomorrow's leg is Deep Lake to Rattlesnake Pass. The men riding the shipment scout and plan their own route.'

Now all eyes turned to examine Steele.

'What do you think, Mr Steele?' the doleful eyed bartender posed.

'That for five thousand dollars, it's worth my while taking a crack at it,' he replied quietly. 'Any of you gentlemen run the grocery store?'

'Me,' a man with a cast in his right eye answered.

'Like to buy supplies for three days,' Steele said.

'Be a pleasure,' the storekeeper replied as if he meant it.

'Which is more than the High Peaks country will be,' somebody growled. 'It's an awful wild place up there.'

His fellow committee members treated the speaker to withering looks.

'Just thought he ought to know,' the culprit said with a shrug.

Steele pursed his lips. 'Grateful to you,' he said. 'I'd like to buy a knife, too. One with good balance.'

'Throwing knife?' somebody asked.

'That's right.'

'No problem, mister.'

'He's got enough of those anyway.'

Steele smiled. 'Man has to take the rough with the smooth,' he said, turning towards the doorway.

The men backed out into the street to leave space for Steele.

'Don't forget what you're going after, mister,' Huntley called, his voice as cold as the wind swirling down the street.

Steele pulled up short of the doorway and looked back over his shoulder. Huntley's face was set in lines that negated every aspect of his apparent character and gave him an air of viciousness.

'Meaning?' Steele asked.

'The men. Not the gold.'

Steele felt anger stretching the skin taut over bones of his face. And his hand took a tighter grip around the Colt Hartford.

Huntley looked sick again and licked his lips hurriedly. 'I've got no reason to trust you, mister,' he muttered.

'Nor any reason not to,' Steele replied tightly.

'That's right, John,' the bartender agreed. 'You wanna ride out into the High Peaks country? Committee'll pay the reward to any man that brings back Street and Duff.'

The offer completely destroyed the hardness which Steele's flash of anger had already undermined. 'I got a job to do here in town,' Huntley said softly.

'Cobbler oughta stick to his last,' the livery stable owner put in.

Steele forced a smile to his lips, to break through the tense lines of his anger. 'Glad you don't want to come along, Huntley,' he said. 'Half of five thousand wouldn't make it worth while for me.'

He went out. The gelding was hitched to a rail, ready saddled and with his bedroll securely lashed in place. The storekeeper had gone on ahead to open up his grocery. The blacksmith sold Steele a knife that felt fine for throwing and fitted snugly into the boot sheath. After stowing the supplies evenly between the two saddlebags, Steele mounted the gelding and looked down into the cold pinched faces of the citizens' committee.

'Dead or alive, Mr Steele,' the bartender said. 'Makes no difference.'

'Maybe not to you,' Steele replied softly.

'Just to them,' the banker said, and the livery stable owner forced a laugh.

'And me,' Steele countered, clucking to his horse and heading the animal across the junction, towards East Street along which the Thorntons and their rescuers had fled.

Chapter Ten

THE biting wind made tracking difficult for it destroyed each hoofprint a moment after it had been formed. And the lack of moonlight added to the difficulty. Clear of the eastern edge of town, Steele dismounted and led the gelding by the reins. He walked with his head stooped, dark eyes swinging from one side of the trail to the other. For a quarter of a mile there was nothing to see. Then fresh horse droppings provided evidence that an animal had gone this way fairly recently. Farther on, higher up the slope of the basin, he found a square of blood-stained fabric, still knotted in the form of a sling. Street had either lost it or decided the dressing hampered his riding.

There was no more sign until he reached the lip of the basin, where he found an irregular row of dark spots against the grey background of the rocky trail. He decided they were blood drops spilled from the reopened knife wound in Street's arm. Or perhaps from an injury one of the Thorntons had received in the explosion at the gaolhouse. But it was immaterial who had dropped the blood on the trail. The spots served to show Steele that the men he was tracking had swung to the north at this point and he gave a grunt of satisfaction as he climbed into the saddle.

Despite his theory about the four men meeting in Endsville to plan a job, he had to allow that it was based on the fragile foundation of a guess. So it had been essential to discover at least one solid fact pointing to the correctness of the theory before heading north.

He no longer looked for signs as he cantered the gelding along the top of the lush pastureland which swept down towards the dark huddle of buildings which formed Endsville. And even when he emerged on to the North Trail he did not waste time with a careful study of the ground ahead. He was better than fifty per cent sure that he was calling the shots right and speed was of the essence now. To either overhaul the four men, or at least get close enough to them to have them in sight before they laid their ambush. They would be in a hurry, too. Not necessarily to stay ahead of possible pursuit: but to get where they were going in time to make contact with the gold wagons. Which meant they would follow the trail as it snaked higher and higher into the mountains. For to veer off to either side would inevitably slow progress considerably.

Steele conserved his own and the gelding's strength, by turns galloping, cantering and trotting the animal. The night grew colder as it grew older and a heavy frost started to fall through the early hours of a new day. He rode with his coat collar turned high and his hat pulled low. Despite the gloves, his hands became numb.

The gloves were as much a bequest from the war as were his skills with gun and knife and his calm approach to death and violence. They had been a present from his father and he had for some inexplicable reason come to regard them as a good luck charm. Always before a battle he had pulled them on: the supple, paper-thin buck-skin in no way interfering with his skill as a marksman. And since the war he had continued to wear the gloves, the act of slipping them on as much a habit as the donning of his hat.

But the luck they brought him was not reliable. He had been wearing them the night he found his father's body swinging on a lynching rope in a Washington barroom. And throughout the violent days which followed, making him as much an outlaw as the men he was now trailing. However, he reasoned to help fill the time as he rode through the cold greyness of a mountain dawn, he was still alive. The threat of sudden death had been lurking close at hand for more than six years and he had survived. If it was irrational to consider the gloves had in some way been responsible for protecting him, then he was prepared to admit that he was a trifle unbalanced. A lesser man might have been driven totally insane by a fraction of the experiences Steele had endured. He knew that some had.

His train of thought was broken just as he was recalling the way in which he had pulled on the gloves prior to riding out of Nuevo Rio. Something caught his eye through the misted breath of the gelding and the ephemeral grey vapour puffing from his own mouth: clear sign on the trail. A jumble of hoofprints stamped on the otherwise virgin white carpet of frost coating the trail. Even as he watched the dark markings, new frost settled to blur them. But they were not entirely obliterated and provided an easy-to-follow course for better than five miles.

By then it was full daylight and the wind had dropped. The eastern sky was clear of cloud and the banking of white immediately overhead and to the west began to roll away, as if fearful of the sun which would shortly rise. The trail was running more or less level now, taking a tortuous route through a landscape of barren, grotesquely weathered outcrops of rock. There was no vegetation anywhere close at hand and Steele was gripped by an eerie feeling that the entire world consisted of nothing but frosted rock.

For long minutes after the sun crested the horizon the mountain land was given a soft, incredibly beautiful look as its rays caused the frost to sparkle. But then the warmth attacked the crystals on the east facing rocks and they became black with damp. A chill mist crept over the land and hovered in a waist-high layer for almost thirty minutes before the sun burned it off. When the trail came back into view again, there was no longer any trace of sign.

Far ahead, Steele could see where the land reared up into a series of jagged ridges, dark on the lower slopes and capped by the solid white of year-long snow above. The mountain tops formed an apparently impassible barrier across the northern horizon and he guessed they formed the area known as the High Peaks country.

He ate breakfast as he rode, of salt beef and crackers. The thought of hot coffee was attractive, but he decided to keep moving until mid-morning, hoping to narrow the gap between himself and his quarry if they called a breakfast halt. There was no kindling for a fire, anyway.

It was from the ridge at one side of a broad, shallow valley that he caught momentary sight of the four men he was tracking. He reined in the gelding and peered the near two miles across the valley which on the far side formed the first step up towards the High Peaks. He saw the four horsemen just as they reached the top of the grade and disappeared beyond. They were no longer on the trail, which ceased to run north at the centre of the valley. Instead, it swung to the west, parallel with the bank of a fast-flowing stream. Scrub grass sprang up at the sides of the stream and there were even clumps of stunted, wind blown trees at intervals along the water course.

The men had rested close to such a grove to feed and water their horses and themselves. A diminishing column of smoke showed where they had failed to douse their fire. Red embers still glowed faintly when Steele rode up to the grove and he fanned them into flame and added fresh twigs to the fire while the gelding chomped on the tough grass. He drank two mugs of coffee fast, then remounted and turned his horse into the white, icy water of the stream. At its deepest, it splashed over his boots and bubbled angrily around the gelding's belly.

The halt had been a short one, but the rest and sparse grazing had done something to revitalise the weary animal and he responded willingly to Steele's order for a steady canter up the long slope. At the top, a leaning column of rock marked the point where the men had gone from sight. When he reached it, the men were still out of sight and there were a dozen natural trails through the high footfalls stepping towards the peaks. Keeping the sun on his right and slightly behind him, Steele guided the gelding due north. For a while, he saw an occasional sign that he had chosen the right route. Hoofprints in a patch of soft earth; a burned out cheroot butt; a drying stain of horse wet or a trail of droppings.

Then the pointers disappeared and he kept pressing ahead on a hunch alone. His route rose and fell by turns, the inclines always steeper than the declines. Despite the sun shining down from a cloudless sky, the still air was intensely cold. And more difficult to breathe as he gained altitude. The thin, very clear air showed him a new sign at mid-day – a black, perfectly straight column of wood smoke standing like a solid pole on a ridge far ahead and to the west of north. The fire was not on the ridge, but beyond it.

Steele held the gelding to a walk as he approached the smoke, conscious of the animal's laboured breathing and tendency to stumble. And when he reached the campsite the quartet of men had left. They had rested in a small hollow among the rocks, the bottom of which was layered with tough grass. The gelding attacked the poor grazing avidly the moment Steele dismounted. There was no kindling and he guessed the men had brought a supply from their last campsite. But there was just enough heat in the embers to warm a pot of water and as he sipped at the tepid coffee, Steele peered up out of the hollow.

The ground sloped up at a steep gradient, formed of solid mountain rock. He guessed he was above the winter snowline now, but at this time of year the first patches of white against grey were another three hundred feet higher. He would be amongst them in less than an hour, on a ridge that looked as if it might be the highest point in the area reachable by men on horseback. For beyond, the peaks seemed to drop away in sheer faces of harsh rock. And if riders could not negotiate such country, how could three heavily laden wagons get through?

Steele sensed he was not alone. The hairs on the nape of his neck prickled and the base of his spine itched. He was being watched from behind and slightly to the left. The gelding, with the stock of the rifle jutting from the boot, chomped grass fifteen feet to his right. Both his gloved hands were wrapped around the meagre warmth of the mug and the flaps of his coat pockets were turned down. He had to trust his judgement on the balance of the knife he had bought in Endsville.

He readied himself in less than a second: then moved in fluid series of reflex actions. He released the mug, powered down into a crouch and spun around, his right hand streaking into the gaping slit of his pants leg. At he drew the knife he was delicately balanced to hurl it at a target and lunge towards the gelding.

'Pity you don't take off your clothes so fast,' Jessica Benson said coldly.

She sat astride a chestnut gelding on the lip of the hollow, looking cold but relaxed. And every inch a woman of experience. Even as Steele allowed the tension to drain out of him and straightened up, he sought the reason for the transformation from false little girl to true woman. Nothing to do with her body, which was thickly encased in warm clothing and showed no curves. The eyes? That had something to do with it. But then he pinned it down. Her blonde hair. The pigtails had been unplaited and the loosened hair fell from under her hat in a cascade of waves, golden in the sunlight. It framed immature prettiness and turned it into sensuous beauty.

'That's the naked truth, Miss Benson,' Steele told her as the woman clucked to her horse and rode him down the slope. He slid the knife back into the sheath.

She halted her horse close to him and he saw how tired were both the animal and the woman. The gelding jerked at the bit to stoop his head to the grass and tore at the feed greedily. The woman eyed the fire, now reduced to grey ashes, regretfully.

'How far away are they?' she asked.

Steele retrieved his discarded mug and waved it up towards the ridge. 'A little more than an hour. You're not just running away then?'

'There's nothing to run away from, Mr Steele. Now that father's dead.'

There was no grief in her tone. She was merely stating a fact. 'What then?' Steele asked as he packed away the mug and checked his cinch.

'Not running to you,' she replied sharply.

'I'll try to keep on living with that knowledge, Miss Benson,' Steele told her softly.

'You'll live a lot longer if you let me help you find them.'

Steele swung up into the saddle and faced her levelly. 'You don't care about me. Is it the money?'

'No. You wouldn't split, anyway. No matter what my father

was, he was my father. If I could be sure you'd bring those men in alive, I'd have stayed in town. But it's not going to be that easy. And I want to see them die.'

She was still very much a woman, but there was no longer anything sexy about her. Her jaw seemed to be carved of the same kind of rock which formed the mountains and her eyes appeared to deepen their shade of green as they mirrored her hate.

Steele held the venomous stare for long moments, then shrugged. 'You've wasted a lot of time not getting what you want, Miss Benson,' he said at length. 'Guess that's made you strong on determination?'

'Besides which?' she posed.

He smiled gently through the stubble of more than twenty-four hours. 'If you've trailed me this far, you'll make it the rest of the way.'

She jerked on the reins to lift her horse's head from the ground. 'Shall we go?'

He led the way out of the hollow and then they rode side by side up the long, steep grade towards the ridge. The going was hard on the geldings and Steele took a zigzagged route, allowing the animals to make their own pace. But the shots changed that.

The rapid fire rifle reports sounded like bursting balloons. But the screams which followed them were of pain rather than excitement. Steele and the woman were within a hundred feet of the snow-powdered ridge when the mountain stillness was shattered by the gunfire. Steele added more noise, yelling into the pricked ears of his mount, jerking on the reins to head the animal straight up the slope and thudding in his heels. The horse snorted and lunged into a gallop. Behind him, Jessica did the same, using the flat of her hand against her mount's back to further encourage him into reluctant speed.

Steele slid the rifle from its boot as he reached the ridge. Close at his heels, Jessica delved a hand inside her bulky coat and drew out a Remington revolver. Steele reined in his horse and the animal skidded to an unsteady halt on a patch of crusted snow. He was at the top of a deep gorge, the ground falling away almost sheer below him to a spring water course.

There was water down there, but it was merely a trickling stream which the three-wagon train had been following. Now the wagons were halted at the narrowest point in the gorge, being fired upon by two men from the front and two from the rear. From where he watched, Steele could clearly see the positions of the ambushers as they sent a hail of bullets towards the wagons. But from ground level the Thornton brothers and Duff and Street would be securely covered by boulders.

At the first moment Steele saw the scene below, the water of the stream was running red with the blood of four dead or wounded men. Two more jerked upwards and were flung back into the water as he watched. Then Jessica Benson hit him. She raced her horse level with his snorting mount, on the side away from the cliff edge. Her hand was curled around the butt of the Remington at the end of an arm thrust out stiffly at right angles to her body. She did not have to swing the arm to add power to the blow. The speed of her horse drove the trigger guard and barrel of the revolver with sickening force into the narrow area of his neck exposed between upturned coat collar and hat brim.

Steele was flung forward against the neck of his mount and the panicked animal reared. His feet slid out of the stirrups and he bounced out of the saddle to thud into the snow. The stream below became a broad river of bright crimson which overflowed to fill the entire gorge. He felt himself being pitched forward into the flood of gore. For the last split second of consciousness, his mind raced.

Jessica Benson had watched him bring the Thorntons into Endsville. Jessica Benson had given him the glad eye and led him into the trap of the alley. Jessica Benson knew John Huntley well enough to prise from him the details of the gold shipment. Jessica Benson did not have the kind of background which would enable her to track men this far into the wild mountains. Jessica Benson had known where to go. Jessica Benson had hit him from behind. Jessica Benson had approached him from the rear before and failed to do just that.

'So you didn't have her,' Steele told himself with the silent voice of his own mind. 'She sure took you.'

Chapter Eleven

THE bay gelding turned as he reared and when he came down there was thin air beneath his lashing forelegs. His belly crashed into the jagged edge of the cliff top and he plunged into the gorge. Every man below heard the animal's cry of pain and fear and looked up. For stretched moments, as the kicking horse dropped, the gunfire ceased. The animal hit a jutting point of rock and died with a broken back. The direction of the carcase's fall was altered by the collision and a man screamed and tried to run. But his foot tripped against an underwater rock and he fell. The dead weight of the animal smashed on top of the man. Human and horse flesh was ripped open by the impact and suddenly the stream was as red as it had seemed in Steele's hallucination.

The horror of pulped flesh and blood-run water was followed by the mild surprise of seeing a woman, blonde hair flying, galloping down the sloping ledge from the top of the cliff. But only the men of the wagon train escort were held by the surprise. To the ambushers, Jessica's appearance on the scene was not unexpected. Thus the Thorntons covering the rear and Street and Duff at the front of the wagons, recovered before the defenders.

A volley of deadly cross-fire spattered along the water course. Two men sheltering under the lead wagon took bullets in their heads. Both pitched face-down into the water. Behind them, a third man was hit in the shoulder and fell sideways. The two horse team started at the sudden renewal of loud noise and backed up. The wagon rolled in reverse and the wounded man was too late in trying to scramble clear of the wheel. It bumped up on to a submerged rock. When it bounced down the iron rim sank clean through the man's right leg, crunching the thigh bone to sever it. He died of shock.

The youngest officer in the escort was crouched behind the crates of gold bullion in the centre wagon. He had a clear shot at Allan Thornton as the fusillade ended and rose to take aim. But this move exposed the back of his head to Arnie Duff. Duff fired and the bullet exploded a spray of blood from the side of the soldier's head. The man was thrown forward over the crates and tipped out over the tailgate to fall into the ice cold water of the stream.

A final burst of fire as Jessica reached the bottom of the gorge finished the fight. Two men under the rear wagon were killed instantly, their bodies riddled with bullets. A lone survivor looked up and down stream through terrified eyes and saw the nine humped forms of his fallen comrades with the blood trails weaving away from them in the flowing water. The man arced his rifle away from him and clambered out on to the seat of the centre wagon thrusting his arms high above his head.

'All right!' he shrieked. 'That's it. I ain't gonna be no hero.'

Duff and Street rose up from behind the boulders, Duff levelling a rifle and Street with a revolver clutched in the hand of his good arm. His other arm was as stiff as Duff's lame leg as both men moved through the shallow water, trailed by the woman on the gelding. The Thorntons emerged from cover a moment later and started to approach the trembling officer from the opposite direction.

Jessica and Allan Thornton grinned at each other and the latter was too interested in the woman to even point his rifle at the soldier. Duff and Street wore satisfied smirks. The elder Thornton rubbed his grizzled jaw and looked at the soldier pensively as the four men and a woman joined into a group at the side of the wagon.

'He sure as hell don't look like no hero,' Fred Thornton said.

'He's shaking,' Street put in.

'Maybe the cold,' Duff suggested lightly.

'Look, you got the gold,' the soldier whined. 'You don't want nothing from me.'

The elder Thornton continued to massage his jaw as he glanced at his brother. Allan was helping Jessica down from her horse with a strange, kind of self-conscious gentleness. 'Only one of us wants a man, and seems to me the lady's got what she wants, soldier boy. See you in hell.'

He casually canted the rifle and shot the man. The bullet entered the soldier's throat and sent a stream of blood from his open mouth before burrowing into the brain and smashing clear through the skull. The body was flipped off the seat and crashed into the water.

'Be a hell of a lot warmer there,' Street growled, holstering the revolver and blowing on his good hand.

Duff looked at Jessica and Allan Thornton just as the couple broke from an embrace. The woman looked at the new corpse with revulsion as Allan giggled. 'Whose horse made the high jump?' he demanded.

'Steele,' Jessica replied.

Street made a hissing sound and clutched at his injured arm. 'The bounty hunter!' he rasped.

Fred Thornton spat into the water rushing around his feet. 'What happened to him?'

'I think I killed him,' Jessica answered.

'You think!' Street roared.

The woman flinched and Allan Thornton put an arm around her. 'I hit him,' she said tightly. 'Very hard.' She pointed upwards. 'Top of the cliff.'

'And you *think* you damn well killed him!' Street roared derisively.

Jessica's green eyes flared with anger. 'I hope I didn't!' she retorted. 'Killing isn't *my* trade.'

'It's all right, honey,' Allan Thornton said softly to her. He glared at Street. 'Lay off her, Dave,' he warned. 'You must have scared the hell out of her in that alley by the hotel. And her old man getting it that way wasn't funny, even if she did hate his guts.'

His brother spat, and the globule splashed into the water between Street's feet. 'Kid's right,' he said harshly. 'What's it matter anyway?'

'It matters,' Street barked, swinging around to face the elder brother. 'I want that bounty hunter dead. And I'm goin' up to make sure he is.'

'It don't matter, Dave,' Duff argued. 'The guy got hit and if he wakes up he's gonna be cold. And he'll get colder. And he won't have a horse or supplies. If he's alive now, he won't be for long.'

'Won't take me long to find out, one way or the other,' Street countered, still clinging to his injured arm. The birthmark at the side of his nose seemed to glow with an inner purple light against the blue-tinged paleness of his face.

'Could be long enough for us to roll these wagons outta here,' Duff replied. 'But I guess you can catch us up.'

As he spoke, he turned away and headed for the lead wagon. He hauled himself aboard. Allan Thornton led the woman's gelding to the rear of the centre wagon and hitched the reins to the tailgate. Then he helped Jessica up to the seat and climbed aloft to sit beside her. His bother went to the rear wagon. Street looked along the line of the wagons, then turned to stare up at the top of the cliff.

'Ain't as hot as hell at the mine,' Duff called. 'But sure a lot warmer than out here, Dave!'

'He better die, that's all!' Street growled, then turned and splashed through the stream to haul himself up beside Duff.

The wagons rolled forward, wheels bursting the unfeeling flesh and crunching the dead bones of the corpses which happened to be in their path. Fifty yards along, where the gorge widened out, Fred Thornton halted the rear wagon and jumped down to fetch the saddle horses from where they had been tethered in a cleft. He hitched them to the back of the wagon and then resumed his position. He yelled at his team to drive them forward in the wake of the other wagons.

It was his raised voice, against the background noise of

splashing hooves and turning wheels, that Steele heard as he regained consciousness. He was sprawled face down in the snow and the coldness against his flesh served to hasten his return to awareness and trigger his memory into total recall. The pain seemed to be a raging fire at every nerve ending, but as his exploring fingers found the swelling at the back of his head, the source was isolated.

Groaning did not help and he contained his suffering in silence as he dragged himself to the edge of the cliff. The water of the stream ran clear again, except where it frothed into foam around rocks and the bodies of the dead soldiers. He looked to his left, along the gorge, in time to see the saddle horses tied to the rear wagon go out of sight around a rock face. Then, when he looked directly below again, he saw that one of the men in the stream was not dead. He was moving, dragging himself to the edge of the trickling and rushing water, sending out red tendrils as his action reopened his wound to spill fresh blood.

Steele rolled over on to his back, sat up and then pushed himself erect. He swayed and the sun, bright without warmth, appeared to zoom back and forth across the sky. But after a moment it held still. He turned and started down the sloping ledge, staggering at first and having to stay close to the gorge wall for fear of going over the edge. But his sense of balance improved with every step. At the foot of the slope he was able to run, until he splashed into the stream and its uneven bed threatened to pitch him into the icy water.

When he reached the injured soldier, the man was at the foot of the gorge wall, sitting up and leaning his back against the rock. Blood was a shiny veil down the left side of his face, spilled from a long wound across his temple. He was trying to point a Colt revolver at Steele, but did not have the strength to bring the muzzle up.

'I've got cold feet already, mister,' Steele said.

The man's drooping eyelids flicked up. 'What?' he murmured.

'If that thing fires at all, it'll shoot water. And you might just manage to squirt some over my boots.'

The man allowed the gun and hand to drop into the water. 'They keep telling up to keep our powder dry,' he groaned before he sank into unconsciousness, his chin dropping on to his chest.

Steele moved in close and squatted down beside the man. Not a man really. A boy of nineteen, perhaps twenty. Clean shaven and with a fresh face where it wasn't masked by blood. Blue eyes and brown hair. A sad mouth. Steele splashed water on the wound and cleaned it enough to see that it was a furrow, not deep enough to have done serious damage. He checked the body and limbs and found no further wounds. It was a slim body and the legs and arms didn't have a lot of meat on them, muscular or otherwise. Even in his weakened state, Steele found it easy to lift the wounded man and carrying him along the water course until the gorge widened enough to provide a dry bank. He lowered his burden gently to the ground, then splashed back into the stream.

He had never seen anything so ghastly as the maggot-infested entrails of Jake Turner. The fleshly dead bodies strewn in the water were no more or less awe-inspiring as many hundred more he had seen in the past. Thus, he was completely detached as he moved among the corpses: and the sight of the merged burst flesh of man and beast left him unmoved. The stock of the Colt Hartford continued to jut from the saddle boot, the inscribed plate glinting in the cold sunlight. He drew the rifle out and saw the blood on the barrel. Water splashes glistened elsewhere. He dunked the barrel and allowed the trickling water to wash away the staining. Then he looked around and found a Spencer rifle and Colt revolver close to one of the dead men. He fished them out and carried all the weapons back to where the injured man was sprawled, breathing shallowly but regularly.

He sat down and stripped all three guns, then used his weighed scarf to wipe dry the disassembled parts. As he was working on putting the Colt Hartford back together again, the young army officer groaned. But it was ten minutes after Steele had finished his chore before the kid was fully back to consciousness and had taken stock of his surroundings.

'Burt Harlan,' he introduced.

'Adam Steele.'

Neither man offered to shake hands.

'Thanks,' Harlan said. He got to his feet and began to tramp

112

up and down a ten pace route, flapping his arms. 'It's cold. But I'd have been stone cold dead if you hadn't pulled me out of the water.'

'You had some luck,' Steele told him.

Harlan nodded. 'The bullet was some of it. But you happening along was the most.' He seemed about to voice a question, but held back. His eyes did the asking.

'I was hired to bring in the men who ambushed the wagons,' Steele supplied. He looked unfeelingly along the stream at the humped forms of the dead soldiers. 'It wasn't specified whether before or after they hit you. Sorry it wasn't before.'

He didn't sound apologetic. But Harlan felt the need to excuse him.

'The spot we were in, one man more or less wouldn't have made any difference.'

He stopped his pacing as the exertion had its effect of restarting the circulation.

Steele nodded to the Spencer and Colt on the stream bank. 'Be grateful if you didn't test them until you're well clear of this area.

Harlan blinked. 'Clear?'

Steele canted the Colt Hartford across his shoulder and nodded along the gorge in the direction the wagons had rolled. 'Still have a job to do. There's no money in it for you.'

Harlan looked along the gorge, then back the other way. Then up the steep walls on either side. 'We're a long way from anywhere, Mr Steele. Those wagons have got supplies aboard. Horses to pull them and canvas to shelter under.'

Steele nodded. 'All right. That way the army still has responsibility for the gold. Happy to have you along, soldier.'

'It's lieutenant,' Harlan corrected as he picked up the two guns, slotting the Colt in his holster.

'That could change if you bring in the gold,' Steele said as he started along the bank of the stream.

Harlan still showed a lot of pain in his eyes, but he managed a grin. 'I never thought about that.'

'Sorry I put the idea in your head, so now forget it,' Steele warned.

'What?' Harlan asked, surprised.

'Concentrate on surviving first. A live lieutenant has just got to be better than a dead captain.'

'I'll stay on my toes when the shooting starts, Mr Steele,' Harlan assured.

'Could be better the other way up, lieutenant,' Steele told him.

'What?'

The bland handsomeness was lit by a grin. 'When the shooting starts. You've got ten toes. Only one head.'

Harlan touched the crusting of congealed blood at his temple. 'They came pretty close once already.' He smiled through his pain once more. 'Guess that makes me a smaller target.' Then he grimaced. 'Why am I grinning. It wasn't funny.'

'Maybe because it creased you,' Steele said.

Chapter Twelve

THE gorge forked a quarter of a mile from where the ambush had taken place, one spur swinging south on a downgrade to take the stream in a headlong rush of white water. The other curved to the north, reaching up to the snowline. South would have been too dangerous for the wagons and Steele and Harlan took the northern spur in tacit agreement that they were on the right track. Up in the snow their guess was proved correct for the prints of hooves and wheels were clearly visible against the sparkling white carpet.

The covering was not thick – no more than six inches except where it had drifted – and had not slowed the wagons very much. They were out of the gorge when they ran into the snow, at the foot of a broad, gentle slope that reached smoothly up towards a razor-backed ridge swept clean of snow by recent winds. They had taken a diagonal course up the slope, leaving an ugly black slash which pointed to the base of a rock face rising in a sheer vertical from the western end of the ridge.

It was late afternoon as Steele and Harlan moved out among the hoofprints and wagon tracks. The sun, which had never been warm, now seemed to be radiating a biting cold. Already the snow was turning to glassy ice where it had been hard-packed by animals and wagons. It made the going difficult and a full thirty minutes had passed by the time the two men had tramped the two hundred feet to the top of the slope. There, sucking in deeply the clear, thin air, they looked down on the objective. They were standing among a hundred shapes and sizes of rocks which had long ago crashed down from the cliff face towering above them. At this end, the ridge was not razor backed. Instead, it broadened to form a small plateau. The ground on the far side fell away in much the same kind of gentle slope as that which they had climbed in the wake of the wagons. But at the bottom there was a difference. Instead of the barren emptiness of snow-covered rock faces there were the remains of a derelict silver mine. Two log cabins flanked a large hole with a sagging framework supporting winding gear straddling it. A winch beside the hole trailed a chain up and over the block and tackle and down into the shaft. Winch and chain were both red with rust.

The wagons had cut a zigzagged course down the slope and were now parked beside the abandoned mine, two of them backed up to the rear of the third. The Thornton brothers and Street and Duff were working hurriedly to transfer all the crates on to one wagon. The whereabouts of Jessica Benson became apparent when grey wood smoke began to curl from the chimney of one of the cabins.

'We got the bastards,' Harlan hissed.

Steele did not respond as he swung his dark-eyed gaze away from the activity below to survey the surrounding terrain, blowing on his gloved hands as he did so. The sloping ground stretched away for at least half a mile in either direction, smooth and virgin white everywhere except for the catty-cornered tracks left by the wagons. Anything moving on the slope could be clearly seen from the old mine workings. Certainly in daylight. And a glance at the sky showed not a trace of cloud as the sun touched the western peaks. It was going to be a moonlit night unless the weather changed rapidly. Not that Harlan and he could risk waiting for dark. Frostbite was too great a danger. And even if they had the time and endurance to circle the old mine, the approaches were exposed on all sides. For it was sited at the side of a broad, shallow valley running down from east to

116

west. The nearest cover, comprised of broken ground, was better than a quarter of a mile away from the workings.

'But they picked themselves a good spot to hole up,' Harlan allowed after making a survey of his own. He was dressed for cold weather in fur-lined boots and thick topcoat, but the clothing was still icily damp from the stream and his face was blue with the cold. 'And we haven't got the time to wait for them to move out,' he added.

'That's a good summary of the problem, lieutenant,' Steele said softly. 'Care to figure out the solution?'

Harlan grinned. 'In the army, a man's got to be at least a major before he starts thinking along those lines, Mr Steele. Anyone below that either delegates or gets delegated.'

Steele gave a non-committal nod which implied he would have done things his own way in any event. 'Soon as they shift all the gold into that one wagon, they'll go inside the shack to eat,' he said, speaking aloud his thoughts. 'They must think everybody back at the gorge was killed – including me.'

'So they won't be expecting callers?' Harlan suggested.

'And might even curb their natural suspicion,' Steele said, watching as the crates were manhandled from one tailgate to another. 'If you had that much gold would you take it easy?'

Harlan grimaced. 'I rode more than a thousand miles with that stuff, Mr Steele. Most of the time through country just as wild as this. If I wasn't watching for trouble, somebody else sure was.'

'So no matter how we go down there, we're going to be spotted.'

Harlan swallowed hard. 'And my head isn't that much less of a target because a bit of it was shot off.'

Both men blew on their gloved hands and continued to watch the Thorntons and Duff and Street shifting the heavy crates. Smoke was rising thickly from the chimney now, smudging a sky that was deepening in colour as the sun sank lower behind the mountains. The cliff under which they stood threw a long shadow, but not deep enough to give cover. And under the darkening sky the snow became crusted with ice which sparkled and seemed to give off a light of its own.

High overhead, an eagle circled, keen eyes raking the wasteland for a clue to its supper. Neither the two men at the top of the slope nor the four at the bottom became aware of the bird until the eagle spotted a possible meal. Then, as it swooped, the flapping of its powerful wings beat against the mountain silence. Human ears were not the only ones to detect the sound. An orphan deer scraping at the snow for the moss beneath looked up and saw the eagle streaking towards it. She was a very young doe who had wandered far from the herd. Already terrified by cold, hunger and loneliness, she was powered into a panicked bolt by the awesome sight of the diving eagle.

She ran blindly from the top of the ridge, bursting out on to the open slope: either not seeing the men at the mine workings or uncaring; seeking only to outrun the giant bird with its clawed talons reaching down for her.

Each man watched in wonder as speed of flight overcame fleetness of foot and the cruel talons of the eagle sank into the back of the deer. Then the viciousness of man took a hand in the necessary anguish of nature. The swooping weight of the bird swept the deer off her feet and thudded her into the snow. The thump triggered a percussion device in the neck of a bottle packed with powder. The powder exploded.

A great spume of snow shot high into the air. It was white on the rise, run with the black of smoke. But as it showered down, the blood of eagle and deer stained it a ghastly crimson. And mixed with it were larger splashes of red as the exploded flesh of bird and animal was scattered across the slope.

'And we were going to rush 'em?' Harlan suggested.

'Were you thinking of doing it that way?' Steele asked as the final pieces of ripped flesh dropped into the awesomely stained snow.

'Better chance than creeping down,' the young army officer said sardonically. 'Now there don't seem any chance.'

Below, the four ambushers were working again, nearing the end of their chore. Steele eyed the zigzagged course of the wagon tracks and realised the pattern had not been assumed solely to reduce the downward cant of the train. The defences of the old mine had been prepared before the ambush took place and the wagons had been veered from side to side to avoid detonating the dormant explosive devices. But Steele discarded the possibility of reaching the mine by the same route. It would more than double the distance between the ridge and the mine. And there was no way of knowing whether or not other booby traps had been laid after the wagons had passed by.

So Steele turned his attention to the rocks among which Harlan and he were concealed. The lieutenant was a bright kid and after watching the stockily-built civilian for a few moments, he guessed the line of thinking behind the unrevealing blankness of the dark eyes.

'We couldn't know if we'd blown every one,' he said.

'We'd soon find out,' Steele replied, counting a dozen roughly spherical boulders big enough to do the job. But not too heavy as to be immovable.

'Bang would go my promotion,' Harlan said. He grinned.

Steele showed him a like expression. 'If you wanted a quiet life, why did you join the army?'

'Because I was born a fool.'

Steele looked around at the cold, bleak mountain terrain and then down at the four men as they completed their task and jumped from the loaded wagon to head for the cabin with the smoking chimney. 'I had to practise a lot,' he said, 'Let's move before we get smart.'

The chosen boulders were spread all over the small plateau and it took them ten minutes to roll them into position, in four ranks of three, spread out across ten yards. Then Steele quickly outlined the plan to Harlan who nodded several times, scared but determined. Both men went forward to check on the situation below. It was twilight now, the sun completely out of sight. A lamp was burning inside the cabin and it looked as warm as it was bright. The horses, still in the traces and hitched to the tailgates, fed from bales of hay which had been dumped in the snow close to them.

'Ready, lieutenant?' Steele asked.

Harlan unbuttoned his coat to expose his holster and tightened his grip on the Spencer. 'As I'll ever be.'

'Let's hope they're not,' Steele said, stooping down to roll the first boulder over the edge.

Harlan followed suit and the next two went into the down slide together. All four made a hissing sound as they tumbled across the snow. Three more were heaved over from the plateau before the first explosion.

Steele and Harlan did not waste time looking at the blast. Instead, they whirled around from the boulders next in line to go, and leapt on to the slope themselves. Another blast crashed and resounded across the terrain as the two men slithered and stumbled in a headlong dash towards the curtain of showering snow. A third, then a fourth. Steele was flung on to his back and slid in the wake of the boulders. Harlan went sideways and was powered into a crazy roll. Fragments of shattered rock zoomed through the artificial snowstorm. Two boulders exploded simultaneously as Steele jarred to a halt in the crater dug by an earlier blast.

As he struggled to his feet and dashed forward to take advantage of the fresh cover of billowing snow, he suddenly realised he intended to kill. Not from hatred nor for self-preservation. To hell with Pedro. To hell with all those staring eyes in Endsville. His job was to bring in Street and Duff. And the Thorntons since they happened to be along. If the positions had been reversed, not one of those four would have any compunction about killing him. Just as if the eagle had been the prey, the doe would not have hesitated to attack with every weapon at its command. But in the animal kingdom, predators killed to eat. The hell with that. A man needed to eat, too. And he needed money to do that. Steele had elected to earn his bread as a bounty hunter. And if the wanted bill stated dead or alive . . . dead made the earning easier.

He saw a shape looming in front of him as another explosion tossed snow and rock chippings into the dark sky of evening. It was one of the empty wagons. It had been blown on to its side by a blast and was rocking violently as the horses in the traces struggled to break free.

'We goddamn made it!' Harlan rasped breathlessly as he flopped down beside Steele in the cover of the overturned wagon.

Both men were coated with clinging snow, from their falls and that which showered down in the explosions.

'We used up a hell of a lot of luck,' Steele rasped softly as the final echo of the last blast faded away into the distance and the horses ceased to struggle.

He looked around and saw that the other empty wagon had also capsized. Its team had broken loose, but the horses had bolted the wrong way. Their ripped open carcasses lay at one end of an enormous blood stain splashed across the snow. The fully laden wagon had been held firm by the weight it carried. Its team were held in the traces. All the saddle horses had scattered.

'It's that damn bounty hunter, I tell you!' Street yelled.

'Just a rock fall, that's all,' Duff countered.

'Rock falls don't start for no reason!' Allan Thornton argued.

'I should have gone and checked on him,' Street snarled.

'Ain't nobody out there, is there?' Duff came back.

'No one I can see,' Fred Thornton replied, and there was the familiar wet sound of a spit. 'But you want to go out and take a look, Arnie?'

There was a pause in the heated conversation and Steele crawled in through a large tear in the canvas covering of the wagon. He found a crack in the floorboards and peered through. The wagon was directly in front of the cabin with the lighted window, with about ten yards separating the two. Nobody was silhouetted at the window and Steele peered to the end of the cabin where he knew the door to be – just out of sight around the angle of the wall.

'If there is anybody, it's Steele,' Jessica Benson said to end the lull. 'All the soldiers are dead, so it's four against one.'

'Oughta be four against none,' Street growled.

'Jesus, there he goes!' This from the elder Thornton as the rapid thudding of running feet on snow sounded.

Steele jerked his head around in time to see Harlan dashing headlong towards the gold wagon. Shots exploded from the cabin doorway and Harlan pitched to the ground, turning and firing as he fell. There was a scream and Street staggered into view, clutching at his chest. Blood spurted from between his fingers and he pitched into the stain it made. Steele swung his gaze back towards Harlan and saw the lieutenant crawl into the insecure cover beneath the wagon as bullets spurted snow around him. He left a trail of blood behind him.

'Make that nine toes!' he yelled as more running footfalls sounded on crisp snow.

Steele drew the knife from the boot sheath as his head swung around. A hail of bullets was streaming from the cabin doorway as Duff made a limping run for the other building on the far side of the mine shaft. Steele flung himself towards the open front of the overturned wagon and hurled the knife. Any sound it made spinning through the thin air was masked by the gun-fire. The blade sank deep into the flesh above Duff's hip. The man staggered to the side. He did not scream until his foot failed to find the ground and he knew he was going into the shaft. He flung aside his rifle and reached for the rusted chain. He missed. His scream was louder within the confines of the shaft. Then diminished into the distant depths. As the gunfire halted, there was a wet sound, rather like Thornton hitting a target with his spittle. But the elder brother was too busy to spit, as he threw down his rifle and drew a sixgun. Allan was engaged in the same act, and Harlan had time to scramble up from the ground and haul himself on to the seat of the wagon. The tightly packed crates of gold were between him and the cabin and bullets smacked ineffectually through timber and flattened against the precious metal.

Under normal circumstances the single team would have been unable to move the overloaded wagon. But with the explosions still ringing in their pricked ears, and gunfire behind them, the horse's strength was augmented by terror. They plunged forward in response to Harlan's yell and the slap of the reins across their backs.

Neither of the Thorntons, nor Jessica Benson, had seen what caused Duff to topple into the mine shaft. Thus, they had no reason to think they had been attacked by more than the single man now driving the gold wagon. They rushed out from cover to give chase. Steele had the Colt Hartford levelled in readiness, the hammer cocked.

The elder brother was in the lead and Steele's first shot exploded through the man's ear, flinging him down like a felled tree. Pieces of flesh and splintered bone trailed after him like scattered foliage. Allan was a yard behind him and had time to swing his head around before Steele's second shot cracked towards him. The bullet swished through his flying fringe and his hair was suddenly a violent red. His dead feet collided with the body of his brother and he pitched across the inert form.

Jessica was the only one to scream, as she tried to stop abruptly and slid across the blood-stained snow. She hit the bodies and sat down hard. Steele straightened up from his crouch and stepped out of the front of the wagon, to move around the snorting horses.

'Lieutenant!' he yelled after the slowly fleeing wagon as he approached the woman.

Harlan leaned to the side to look back, and grinned at the sight which greeted him. He hauled over on the reins to turn the wagon.

'And to think I could have killed you,' Jessica sobbed, turning her gaze from the blood-run head of the younger Thornton to stare hatefully up at Steele.

'Know how you feel, Miss Benson,' he replied softly. 'I could have taken care of the Thorntons in Mexico and the other two in Endsville. Saved myself a lot of trouble. But you have to take the rough with the smooth. Learn by your mistakes.'

'If ever I get the chance again –'

The gold wagon exploded. Harlan had turned it the wrong way but he couldn't know the right one. The team missed stepping on the detonator, but the front offside wheel found it. The wagon was smashed over on to its side as the horses were blasted from the traces. Harlan sailed into the air amid a shower of snow. Crates of gold spilled out and one crashed down upon another hidden bottle of powder. Blocks of gold rocketed into the air and thudded into Harlan's falling body. As he hit the ground some of the bars were still sunk into the gaping wounds they had made.

Steele and the woman were both blown off their feet by the force of the blast. Steele was hurled into soft snow, head first. He rolled over and sprang into a crouch, swinging the rifle, recalling Jessica's warning. But he could not see where her body had fallen. Then, diminished by the echo of the twin explosions, he heard that distant wet sound for the second time that night – like Fred Thornton spitting. And he knew where Jessica Benson was.

He canted the rifle across his shoulder as he straightened up, listening to the silence. The moon was up now and, as he had guessed, it reflected brightly on the stained snow. It provided more than enough light for him to examine the overturned wagon with the team still hitched. It was still sound and the team could be used to set it back on its wheels. He didn't have to examine Harlan closely to know the lieutenant was dead. Nor did he bother with the gold. Like Harlan and the other soldiers back at the gorge, that was the army's problem.

His own problem? To take Duff and Street back to Endsville and claim the reward. True, he had not killed Street. But then he had not killed Jake Turner in Nuevo Rio and had still collected. Not only a predator. Also a scavenger.

He didn't think about it for too long. That was the way. Not to think. At least, to try not to think.

For a while, there wasn't time, as he unhitched the team, whispering gently to them. Then rehitching them to the side of the wagon and urging them forward to pull it over into an upright position. Finally, back into the traces.

He loaded Street's body aboard, ignoring the Thornton brothers. Then he went to the winch and began to turn the handle. He was fully prepared to go down the shaft for Duff, but it didn't prove necessary. It was a deep shaft and a lot of chain was wound in before a hook appeared. To the hook were fastened four lengths of short chain, attached to the corners of a six-wheeled truck. The crushed, pulpy body of Duff hung over one side of the truck and Jessica Benson was curled in the centre of the truck, shards of broken bone piercing through the clothing which hid her once voluptuous body. Blood sloshed in the bed of the truck at Steele hauled Duff's corpse clear. He dragged it across to the wagon and hoisted it up and over the tailgate. Then he returned to the head of the shaft and looked at the broken body of the woman.

'You wanted to get out of town, Miss Benson,' he said, touching the brim of his hat. 'So you wouldn't thank me for taking you back. At least you saw what's on the other side of the mountains. For you, it comes out the same . . . ' He kicked the ratchet out of engagement and the winch spun free. The weight of the truck and its grisly contents played out the chain at a tremendous speed. Rust particles billowed. The truck hit the bottom of the shaft with a distant crash – tiny in comparison with the recent explosions.

' . . . ENDSVILLE.'

But not for Adam Steele. Watch out for No. 3 in the series.

EDGE: THE LONER
by George G. Gilman

First in a new Western series whose hero is the lone and sinister Edge – a new kind of Western hero, a man alone.

The idealised Westerner lives clean, is respectful to ladies, courteous to his social inferiors and gives his enemies a sporting chance.

Edge is not an idealised Westerner – not in any way at all.

Look out for Edge.

NEW ENGLISH LIBRARY

NEL BESTSELLERS

T011 682	ESCAPE ON VENUS	Edgar Rice Burroughs	40p
T013 537	WIZARD OF VENUS	Edgar Rice Burroughs	30p
T009 696	GLORY ROAD	Robert Heinlein	40p
T010 856	THE DAY AFTER TOMORROW	Robert Heinlein	30p
T016 900	STRANGER IN A STRANGE LAND	Robert Heinlein	75p
T011 844	DUNE	Frank Herbert	75p
T012 298	DUNE MESSIAH	Frank Herbert	40p
T015 211	THE GREEN BRAIN	Frank Herbert	30p

War

T013 367	DEVIL'S GUARD	Robert Elford	50p
T013 324	THE GOOD SHEPHERD	C. S. Forester	35p
T011 755	TRAWLERS GO TO WAR	Lund & Ludlam	40p
T015 505	THE LAST VOYAGE OF GRAF SPEE	Michael Powell	30p
T015 661	JACKALS OF THE REICH	Ronald Seth	30p
T012 263	FLEET WITHOUT A FRIEND	John Vader	30p

Western

T016 994	No. 1 EDGE – THE LONER	George G. Gilman	30p
T016 986	No. 2 EDGE – TEN THOUSAND DOLLARS AMERICAN		
		George G. Gilman	30p
T017 613	No. 3 EDGE – APACHE DEATH	George G. Gilman	30p
T017 001	No. 4 EDGE – KILLER'S BREED	George G. Gilman	30p
T016 536	No. 5 EDGE – BLOOD ON SILVER	George G. Gilman	30p
T017 621	No. 6 EDGE – THE BLUE, THE GREY AND THE RED		
		George G. Gilman	30p
T014 479	No. 7 EDGE – CALIFORNIA KILLING	George G. Gilman	30p
T015 254	No. 8 EDGE – SEVEN OUT OF HELL	George G. Gilman	30p
T015 475	No. 9 EDGE – BLOODY SUMMER	George G. Gilman	30p
T015 769	No. 10 EDGE – VENGEANCE IS BLACK	George G. Gilman	30p

General

T011 763	SEX MANNERS FOR MEN	Robert Chartham	30p
W002 531	SEX MANNERS FOR ADVANCED LOVERS	Robert Chartham	25p
W002 835	SEX AND THE OVER FORTIES	Robert Chartham	30p
T010 732	THE SENSUOUS COUPLE	Dr. 'C'	25p

Mad

S004 708	VIVA MAD!		30p
S004 676	MAD'S DON MARTIN COMES ON STRONG		30p
S004 816	MAD'S DAVE BERG LOOKS AT SICK WORLD		30p
S005 078	MADVERTISING		30p
S004 987	MAD SNAPPY ANSWERS TO STUPID QUESTIONS		30p

NEL P.O. BOX 11, FALMOUTH, TR10 9EN, CORNWALL
  Please send cheque or postal order. Allow 10p to cover postage and packing on one book plus 4p for each additional book.

Name ....

Address..

....

Title ....
(SEPTEMBER)